Benny Feldman's All-Star Klezmer Band

To Lois, our dear friend

Benny Feldman's ♫ All-Star ♫ Klezmer Band

Allison and Wayne Marks

Green
Bean
Books

Green Bean Books

First published in 2020 by Green Bean Books,
c/o Pen & Sword Books Ltd,
47 Church Street, Barnsley, S. Yorkshire, S70 2AS
www.greenbeanbooks.com

Paperback edition: 978-1-78-438555-2
Harold Grinspoon Foundation edition: 978-1-78-438559-0

Library of Congress Cataloging-in-Publication Data available

Typeset in Garamond 12/16
by JCS Publishing Services Ltd, www.jcs-publishing.co.uk
Printed and bound by CPI Group (UK) Ltd, Croydon, CR0 4YY

MIX
Paper from
responsible sources
FSC® C020471

♪ 1 ♪

Ms. Krumholtz's voice jolted eleven-year-old Benny Feldman from his early-morning fog. The sixth-grade class in Room 610 settled down as she read the morning announcements: "Bring in your cans for the winter food drive. Let's beat those seventh-graders this year! Don't forget that Monday is our field trip to the Geary Potato Chip Factory. Your personal essays are due next week—absolutely no extensions!"

It looked like the start of another typical day at Sieberling School. And that was okay with Benny. Typical was predictable. Typical meant he might be able to make it through the next seven hours without drawing unwanted attention.

Ms. Krumholtz's final piece of news made Benny's heart race like a metronome stuck on warp speed. "I almost forgot. The school talent show will be happening in March. The sign-up sheet will be posted on the bulletin board next to the library."

So much for typical, Benny thought.

The class erupted into chatter. Amanda Grayson, who sat to Benny's right, squealed with delight. She had been twirling batons since the age of two. At least once an hour she mentioned a video of her performance at the Regional Junior Majorette Competition. Flipping her purple marker in the air, she caught it behind her back without looking, spun it between her fingers, and turned to Benny.

"97,838 views," Amanda said, monitoring the video's popularity on her phone. "Are you going to be in the talent show this year? Of course, that would mean you *have* some kind of talent."

Does she have to say that to me every year?

In fifth grade Amanda had won second place with her "Star-Spangled Salute to the Presidents."

"Wait until you see my new routine," she said. "So what's your answer? Are you going to be in the talent show or not?"

Benny's face turned crimson and his palms began sweating. He started to reply but then shrugged and buried his face in his science book, pretending to be fascinated by the properties of sedimentary rocks.

To Benny's left, Jason Conroy bragged about his new electric guitar. "It's a Gibson Flying V with a wicked psychedelic design on the front," he said, cradling a notebook and pretending to strum it while his left hand moved up and down an imaginary fretboard. He glared at Benny, who froze like a startled deer in Jason's blue-eyed headlights. Dropping his head, Benny stared at a diagram of the water cycle.

"Remember how my band rocked the house last year?" Jason said. "I'll be sure to save you a seat in the front row next to all my other *adoring fans*. You're coming to the talent show, right?"

Benny nodded and returned to his textbook.

Avoiding the talent show was not an option. Sam, Benny's nine-year-old brother, snagged third place last year with his juggling act. The crowd gave him a standing ovation for keeping two apples and a banana in the air for three minutes while hopping on one foot. Now in fourth grade, Sam had been working on adding a kiwi to his routine.

Benny's parents would never allow him to skip the show unless he was sick. Really sick. Head-in-the-toilet sick. He started practicing fake coughs when the bell rang.

≳ ♪ ≲

In the art room, Benny concentrated on molding a lump of clay into a menorah. If he finished it on time—and if it *looked* like a menorah—he planned to give it to his parents for Hanukkah, which was a couple of weeks away. Right now the clay resembled a nine-tentacled sea creature ill-equipped to hold a shamash candle. His best friend, Ollie Broadleaf, kneaded his clay into a nutcracker. He was easily the most talented artist in the school.

3

"You really are a master at sculpting," Benny said. "Seriously, that looks just like the figurines at the mall gift shop. You're the class Michelangelo."

"Thanks, your octopus is pretty great, too," Ollie said.

Benny laughed. "It's supposed to be a menorah. You know, the special candleholder used during Hanukkah."

"Well, that's the most exceptional Hanukkah octopus I've ever seen."

"I guess sculpting isn't my thing."

From the far end of the long table, Jason perked up his ears. "So what *is* your thing?" he asked. The room went silent. All eyes bored into Benny.

Here we go again.

Jason repeated the question, his voice rising. "You heard me. What *is* your thing? What can you actually *do*?"

Benny's eyes watered behind his thick black-rimmed glasses. His throat tightened as the class awaited his response. He said nothing.

"Mind your own business!" Ollie shouted. Benny bowed his head and aimlessly poked at his misshapen project.

♪

For the rest of the school day, Benny relived Jason's taunts. When the final bell rang, he looked forward to the solitude of his room at home.

Passing by the library on his way out of school, Benny glanced at the talent show sign-up sheet. Rappers, poets, comedians, actors, gymnasts, and ballet dancers filled the lines. At the top, his food-juggling brother had scrawled "Sam Feldman's Flying Fruits." Below that in slanted letters was Jason's band, "The Neanderthal Four," followed by "Amanda Grayson's Twirling Tribute to the Fifty States."

Benny stared at the last few empty lines and reached for a black felt-tip marker in his back pocket.

"Hurry up!" a girl shouted. "Are you just going to stand there? My bus leaves in five minutes."

This is an awful idea. A monumental mistake. A disaster of catastrophic proportions, Benny told himself. He began to put the marker away when a familiar voice made him stop cold.

"Don't worry, folks. Benny can't do anything—other than be the Amazing Exploding Grape."

It was Jason. He had given Benny this nickname in first grade. Over time the name had faded until Benny thought it had disappeared. But everything had changed last year. Now Benny couldn't go a day without someone bringing back the name that wouldn't go away.

Hearing Jason in the crowded hallway and the laughter that followed pushed Benny over the edge. *That's it! No more! I will not be watching you from the front row. And I will not let your band win this year!*

In one swift motion Benny uncapped the marker and wrote in capital letters: BENNY FELDMAN'S ALL-STAR KLEZMER BAND.

Stepping back, he stared in disbelief. He had broken

his number-one rule for how to survive school: Blend into the background.

What have I done? Benny thought. *What have I done?*

♫ **2** ♫

Benny slammed the door to his room. He wondered if it would be possible to hit the delete key on the last few hours. Images from the day streamed through his brain— over and over again. Flying V guitars. Batons. Squishy menorahs. Kiwis. His name written in bold capital letters.

Since first grade, Benny had been compiling a mental list of rules for getting through the day. It included everything from "Homeroom survival tips" to "Cafeteria gravy is not actual food." In the evening he often turned to a rule that never let him down: When in doubt, play your violin.

He took out the instrument and guided the bow across its strings. Rollicking klezmer tunes with names none of his classmates could even begin to pronounce filled the room: "Der Heyser Bulgar" and "Lebedik un Freylekh." He had memorized them and a hundred more, note for note. All felt like good friends. Klezmer—instrumental Jewish music from Eastern Europe—was Benny's escape, his secret, his *thing*. It had always been safe from teasing and out of reach of Jason Conroy.

As he fiddled, Benny imagined himself standing straight and tall, leading a famous klezmer band like the ones on the old records he collected. Behind him a drummer kept a steady beat. An accordionist squeezed sweet chords from the instrument's bellows. The clarinetist's high notes rose above the cheering crowd, who clapped and danced in a circle as the music swirled to a feverish conclusion. His vision always ended the same, with the audience begging for an encore.

Until now, Benny Feldman's All-Star Klezmer Band had only existed in Benny's head, where he believed it would stay forever.

He gently laid the fiddle in its blue-velvet-lined case and covered it with a checkered cloth.

This is what I can do, Jason, he thought. *But putting together a klezmer band good enough to win the talent show? In a few months? How in the world am I going to make that happen?*

♪

Mrs. Feldman plopped a big spoonful of sliced zucchinis and mushrooms onto Benny's plate, the final insult to a terrible day. Benny hated zucchinis and mushrooms almost as much as he disliked Jason. Almost.

"Did you hear that Sam is going to be in the talent show again?" Mr. Feldman asked.

"So is Benny!" Sam said. "His klezmer band is going to perform."

Mrs. Feldman dropped the serving spoon. Benny kicked Sam under the table.

"Is that true?" Mr. Feldman asked softly.

"It's true! I promise!" Sam said. "His name is on the sign-up sheet. Benny Feldman's All-Star Klezmer Band."

"I want to hear it from Benny, please," Mr. Feldman said. He knew about Benny's stage fright, and he was fairly certain Benny did not have his own band.

After a long pause, Benny raised his head. "Yes, I did it."

"See? See? I told you!" Sam said. "Benny's going to be right up there on stage. In … front … of … EVERYBODY! How cool is that? That makes two Feldmans in the talent show!"

Benny did not appreciate Sam's outburst or his enthusiasm. The thought of getting on stage—in front of EVERYBODY—made him squirm. He kicked Sam again, twice as hard.

"Ouch! What did I say?"

"That's enough," Mrs. Feldman said. She turned to Benny and placed her hand on his arm. "Tell us what happened."

"I'm not sure. I couldn't stop myself. Now I'm signed up to perform…."

"… in a band that doesn't exist," Mr. Feldman said, finishing Benny's sentence. "If it makes you that upset, just erase your name from the list. Then nobody will know you signed up."

Too late. I wrote my name in ink. Pencil can be erased, but ink is forever, Benny thought.

Besides, his brother knew. Jason knew. Benny assumed that, thanks to social media, the news would spread everywhere, from the kids in Room 610 to the weekend anchors on CNN. He pictured the President retweeting his announcement.

"There *is* another option," Mrs. Feldman said. "Show the world what a fine musician you are. I'm sure you could find some classmates to join you."

Benny could not imagine that Sieberling School was swarming with kids who shared his passion for playing soulful *doinas* or festive *freylekhs.*

I doubt my classmates would join me in anything. At Sieberling there are popular kids like Amanda and Jason, everyone else, and me.

"Think about it over the weekend," Mr. Feldman suggested.

Benny's phone vibrated in his pocket. The screen showed a text from Ollie.

Thx for telling me you were in a band. Aren't we best buds?

Sorry, he texted under the table. Long story.

♫ **3** ♫

November leaves crunched beneath Benny and Ollie's feet as they walked by the 100-year-old homes in Benny's neighborhood. In the business district, they passed Ritzberg's Pharmacy, Fernando's Frozen Custard, the Highland Coffee House, and shops selling everything from vintage clothing to aquarium supplies.

Side by side, Benny and Ollie resembled a pair of mismatched bookends. Ollie was short and slightly pudgy, with closely cropped red hair and a roundish freckled face. Benny was the tallest in his class, which made blending in an impossible task. He had curly black hair and unusually long fingers. "You have a fiddler's hands, like Paganini," his Uncle Maxwell had commented at Benny's first violin lesson five years ago.

Benny and Ollie had met at the beginning of sixth grade. Ollie was the new kid looking for a friendly face. Benny was the kid who had grown used to eating lunch alone in the cafeteria. Their discussions revolved around

Star Trek vs. Star Wars, favorite cartoons, and which gaming consoles were best for blasting zombies. Benny helped Ollie with spelling and subject/verb agreement. Ollie gave Benny tips on drawing in perspective and dividing fractions.

Every Tuesday Benny and Ollie went to the park to play frisbee. On Saturdays they mowed lawns and raked leaves to earn spending money. Benny liked having someone he could call a friend. It made sixth grade bearable. He also liked Ollie because he didn't ask a lot of questions—until today.

"Where are you taking me?" Ollie asked.

"Trust me. You'll love it," Benny said.

Down a side street they stopped in front of Alistair's Oddities. It was Benny's favorite hangout. The one-room shop was packed with old *Popular Mechanics* magazines, fossils, foreign coins, 35-millimeter cameras, and political buttons dating back to the 1930s. Teardrop mandolins, movie posters, framed collections of exotic insects, and other garage-sale finds crowded the walls. The room smelled of must and strong coffee. Benny and Ollie were greeted by a lively Scottish tune coming from a record player on the front counter.

Alistair Wilkins, the owner, broke into a broad grin when he saw the pair enter. "BENNNNNNY!" he cried. "Nice to see you! Who's your sidekick?" Lanky and gaunt, Alistair had long gray hair pulled back into a ponytail.

He wore his year-round outfit, a tie-dyed shirt and white carpenter pants.

"Alistair, meet Ollie," Benny said. Ollie gave a slight wave, his eyes drawn to a 1960s pinball machine lit up in the corner.

"Anything new?" Benny asked.

"You're in luck. I picked up a few goodies at an estate sale last week. Check them out."

Benny went straight to the peach crates jammed with old 78 record albums. He thumbed through them, pausing at a disc in a plain white paper sleeve. The title on its blue label read, "Tantz, Tantz Yiddelech / Abe Schwartz's Orchestra." Covered with scratches and smudged with fingerprints, the record looked as if it hadn't spun on a turntable in more than eighty years.

"Mind if I put this on?" Benny asked, blowing a puff of dust off the vinyl surface and wiping it with a cloth.

"Be my guest," Alistair said.

When the needle on the vintage turntable touched the first groove, the dormant record sprang to life. It crackled and spat before emitting a stream of high-pitched fiddles and chirping clarinets. Drums and tubas boomed in the background while the melody played for over three minutes. The furious rush of instruments poured out of the record player's small, tinny speaker.

To Benny, it was a chorus of angels. He closed his eyes and tapped out a quick rhythm with his right foot as he mimed playing a violin to the music.

From Ollie's perspective the tune sounded like feral cats fighting in a burlap sack. He preferred listening to speed metal and hip-hop, with an occasional classic rock song thrown in. Klezmer would never find its way onto Ollie's phone, but if Benny liked it, that was fine with him.

After the last note faded, Ollie could only think of one thing to say: "How about some pinball?"

Alistair had rigged the machine so customers could play for free as long as they wanted. It had been in his family since his eleventh birthday and was the only item in the shop not for sale.

A winking genie painted onto the machine's back glass stared at Ollie. He pulled back the plunger and sent the metal ball rocketing up the chute. It hugged the curved top rail before pinging between three 100-point bumpers arranged in a triangle.

"So *that's* klezmer?" Ollie asked, working the flippers to keep the ball in action. "That's what your band plays?"

"Yes, that's klezmer," Benny said. "But no, my band doesn't play it … because there is no band. I'm a fiddler for real, but I made up Benny Feldman's All-Star Klezmer Band."

"Then why did you write it on the sign-up sheet?" Ollie groaned as his ball disappeared down the center between the bottom flippers.

Benny took his turn at the machine. "I finally had enough of Jason's teasing. I had to do something. Now

I'm stuck. I don't have a band and I'm terrified of performing in front of people. Jason will do everything he can to make sure he wins again."

"What's his problem with you?" Ollie watched Benny's nimble fingers send the ball wherever he wanted, racking up points by the second as the machine's white and black mechanical numbers flipped over.

"Jason and I used to be best friends. Our families carpooled to Sunday school together."

"Jason is Jewish, too?"

"Uh-huh. I see him at school during the day and I have to avoid him at synagogue." The thought made Benny hit the flippers harder. "We did lots of stuff together."

"What happened?"

"On the soccer team, Jason scored the goals; I'd lose the game when the ball went through my legs. In T-ball, he'd hit the home runs; I'd strike out with the bases loaded."

"Strike out? In T-ball?" Ollie asked.

"Yes, T-ball. I couldn't even hit a ball that wasn't moving. Jason hates losing. I guess he got tired of hanging out with a loser."

"First off, you're not a loser. And I still don't get why you're not friends anymore." Benny caught the ball on the right flipper, let it roll to its tip and then flicked it to the left.

He flipped the silver ball against a triangular slingshot, sending it ricocheting and crisscrossing around the machine. It set off an explosion of bells and buzzers. When he finished, he had 9,999 points, the machine's highest score. Benny sent another ball into play.

"I haven't told you about the Sunday school class play. I've never talked about it with anyone."

"Was it that bad?"

Benny tensed his hands as the ball slid by the flippers and into the belly of the table. "Worse than you can imagine."

♪ **4** ♪

Back in first grade, Benny burst into the house with big news. His Sunday school class was putting on a Sabbath play, and he had been cast in one of the most important roles.

"I get to be the Fruit of the Vine," he said to his parents. "Jason is going to be the Bread from the Earth. We both have lines to learn and get to wear costumes!"

"How exciting!" Mrs. Feldman said.

"Super!" Mr. Feldman added. "What are your lines?"

Benny produced a piece of paper from his Beth El tote bag. He smoothed the creases and read in a clear voice, "Behold, I am the Fruit of the Vine!" Then he bowed.

His parents cheered as Sam hugged his brother's legs.

At Sunday school the class rehearsed on the stage in the reception hall. The Grossman twins, Clara and Ethan, portrayed the Sabbath Candles. Karen Neumar played the Kiddush Cup. The rest of his classmates would lead the congregation in reciting the Sabbath prayers and singing songs. The finale was a dance choreographed by their teacher, Mrs. Mandelbaum.

At home the Feldmans worked on Benny's costume. Mrs. Feldman made a robe out of purple felt. Mr. Feldman sewed a brown cap with a pipe-cleaner stem poking out from its center. Sam helped to shop for purple makeup to cover Benny's face and grape-colored balloons to blow up and attach to the costume on the day of the performance.

Benny wiggled into the felt robe, put on the cap, and admired himself in front of the mirror. He could hardly wait for Friday night services. All his aunts, uncles, and cousins would be in the audience, along with friends from school lured by the promise of free cookies and pastries afterwards.

Trouble started at the final practice when a disagreement broke out between Jason and Benny. Jason claimed that bread was far more important than grapes.

"Without bread, there wouldn't be sandwiches," Jason said. "And without sandwiches, there'd be no peanut butter and jelly." He crossed his arms and smirked, satisfied with his logic.

"But without grapes, there wouldn't be grape juice," Benny countered. "Who wants to eat a dry sandwich without something to wash it down?"

"Bread!" Jason shouted.

"Grapes!" Benny replied.

"Bread!"

"Grapes!"

"Bread, bread, bread, bread, bread!"

"Grapes, grapes, grapes, grapes, grapes!"

They argued back and forth until Mrs. Mandelbaum stepped in. "You are both equally important," she said, rolling her eyes.

Unconvinced, the two had stopped speaking to each other by the end of practice.

On Friday morning Benny awoke with a sore throat. By the end of school, the tickle on his tonsils had blossomed into a full-blown head cold. His nasal passages were as congested as the cafeteria line on pizza day.

"I'll be fibe. Ebryone is counting on be. I can't biss it," he pleaded.

"I'm not sure if this is a good idea," Mrs. Feldman said as they prepared to leave.

"The play only lasts for half an hour," Mr. Feldman reasoned. "What could go wrong?"

Backstage, Benny compared his costume to the others. As the Kiddush Cup, Karen sported a plastic bowl on her head painted silver and decorated with sparkles. The Grossman twins wore gold pants for the candlesticks, white shirts for the candles, and orange cardboard flames attached to headbands. Benny thought Jason had the best costume. His head, arms, and legs poked out of a papier-mâché challah so realistic a preschooler tried to take a bite out of it.

The curtain opened to enthusiastic clapping. Covered in heavy felt and twenty balloons, Benny did his best to stay upright. The hot stage lights caused the thick purple makeup on his face to run into his eyes. Trapped in his private sauna, he wobbled but managed to say his line at the right time.

"Behobe, I am the Frube of da Bine," he said through clogged sinuses.

Jason, Karen, and the Grossman twins recited their lines perfectly, followed by the crowd saying the prayers and singing along to the Sabbath songs.

Only a few minutes had passed, but it seemed like a lifetime to Benny. *I'm going to make it! I'm going to make it!* he thought.

Then came the dance.

Everyone held hands and skipped in a circle singing, "Shabbat is finally here, my friends. Shabbat is finally here!" But after the second rotation, the room began to spin and Benny lost his grip on the Kiddush Cup's hand. Let loose from his classmates' orbit, he flailed his arms and whirled close to the edge of the stage.

"Go, Benny, go! That's my brother!" Sam shouted.

Benny careened into the Sabbath candle twins, knocking them into the Bread from the Earth. Jason dropped on his back and helplessly rocked like a box turtle unable to turn over. Benny collided with Karen the Kiddush Cup, sending her sprawling on top of the floundering challah. The impact bounced Benny off the back wall, causing the balloons on his outfit to explode like a string of firecrackers.

Babies screamed.

Rabbi Stieglitz clutched his chest.

The entire first row ducked for cover.

Benny teetered off the stage and threw up as Mrs. Mandelbaum jerked the curtain closed.

Sitting alone backstage, Benny watched the cast troop past him without saying a word. Jason waddled over to Benny and looked him square in his purple-stained face. "You ruined everything," he said. "I'll never let you forget this. I'm not your friend anymore!"

$$\gtrless \, \text{♫} \, \lessgtr$$

"And we haven't been friends since," Benny said, tucking the "Tantz, Tantz Yiddelech" record under his arm and heading to the cash register. "There's one thing Jason hates even more than losing—being embarrassed."

"I had no idea," Ollie said as they left Alistair's Oddities. "You have to admit, it's kind of a funny story." Benny's stony face immediately made Ollie regret his words.

"Not to me," Benny said. "It will never be funny."

"Sorry, man. But Jason can't still be mad at you about the play?"

"No. He made new friends and learned the guitar. He put together an awesome band. He got over the play, but he never completely forgot about it."

"How do you know?"

Benny didn't answer.

"Are you jealous of him?"

Maybe a little, Benny thought. "No, I just want him to leave me alone."

"Well, you have me," Ollie said. "That's not going to change."

The two bumped fists. "Thanks. The same goes for me. Anyway, since the play, I haven't been able to go on stage—I just think it's all going to happen again. I even manage to avoid standing up in front of the class. It's easier that way."

"Now you don't have a choice."

"I know."

"Any idea who you'll get to be in your band?"

"I don't have a clue."

As Benny opened the door to enter his house, Ollie called from the sidewalk: "I still don't get why Jason teases you. I mean, the play was FIVE years ago."

"Gotta go, Ollie. See you Monday."

♪

That night, Benny felt guilty about lying to Ollie—and to himself. Benny wasn't just a little jealous of Jason. He was green with envy, a shade somewhere between emerald and deep forest. Whenever they competed against each other, Jason always came out on top. Benny could remember every detail of every defeat, no matter how small. Alone in the dark, Benny recalled a few memories from his long list:

First grade: Rachel Bidlingmyer's sixth birthday party—Jason pins tail on donkey; Benny pins tail on Rachel's forehead.

Second grade: Gym—Jason climbs rope like a squirrel monkey; Benny dangles ten inches off the floor.

Third grade: Day camp—Jason captures the flag; Benny captures a summer-long case of poison ivy.

Fourth grade: Room 421—Jason is elected classroom president; Benny receives a single vote (his own), finishing one behind Spike, the class pet iguana.

Then there was fifth grade. Benny hadn't told Ollie what happened during the class picnic, the day Jason started calling him the Amazing Exploding Grape again. Whenever Benny passed the basketball courts at Ardmore City Park, his mind replayed the incident in slow motion. It was a story Benny wasn't ready to tell, even to his best friend.

Before drifting off to sleep, Benny thought about Jason's words: *What can you actually do?* It wasn't the first time Jason had said it. As Benny turned off the light, he was determined to make sure it would be the last.

♩5♪

Benny's violin lesson began as always.

"Scales first. No dessert until you eat your vegetables," Uncle Maxwell said, removing his brown fedora and using a red bandana to wipe sweat from his bald head.

Benny knew what this meant. Scales, repetitive bowing studies, and finger exercises were the peas, carrots, and spinach of the lesson. The klezmer tunes he loved were the big slice of chocolate cake at the end. Today, though, everything tasted like cooked zucchinis and mushrooms.

Benny removed his fiddle from its case. Its top plate was crafted from brown spruce wood. The back, made from flamed maple, had a striped pattern like a jungle cat. He twisted its ebony tuning pegs until the sound from all four strings pleased his ear.

"Ready?" Uncle Maxwell asked, stroking his long black beard. "Let's begin with an *Ahava Raba* scale."

Benny could play this in his sleep—a spicy progression of notes as recognizable to him as sauerkraut on a Reuben sandwich. The scale formed the basis for many of his favorite klezmer tunes. He played a low E, taking a full bow stroke from frog to tip. When he reached the fiddle's upper range, he effortlessly walked his fingers back down like a spider spinning a silken web.

One helping of vegetables done, he thought.

Five more warm-up scales followed. When told to play his finger exercise, Benny gazed at the page blackened with notes. Usually he attacked these challenging passages with gusto, but his lack of enthusiasm signaled to his uncle that something was wrong.

"You're playing the notes, but I sense your head is somewhere else," Uncle Maxwell said. "Spill it."

Benny hesitated. He had already unloaded his problem on Ollie and his parents, so he wanted to spare his uncle the story.

"Come on. Your uncle has heard it all before."

"Nobody can help."

"Try me."

If you insist. Benny made it brief, condensing his tale of woe into one sentence blurted out in a single breath: "I signed up to play my violin in the school talent show."

"*Mazel tov!*" Uncle Maxwell said, both thrilled and shocked at the announcement. He had attended the Sabbath play and knew Benny kept his fiddling a secret. "Do you have a tune in mind?"

"It's not that simple," Benny said, laying his fiddle

back in its case. "I signed up to play in a *band*—Benny Feldman's All-Star Klezmer Band!"

"I see. That does make it more complicated. I'm assuming your school doesn't have a thriving klezmer club."

"Hardly."

"I know lots of musicians who could sit in with you. Heck, I could join you myself."

Benny had considered this. He had seen his uncle perform many times at weddings and family gatherings. "Thanks, but *if* I go through with this, I need to do it myself."

"I understand."

"And even if I find a band, I'm not sure … you know…."

"Yes, I know."

"Also, I'm afraid the kids at school will think klezmer is weird … that I'm weird … or weirder than they already think I am. What if I … we … whoever … gets booed off the stage? Being different is hard."

"Yes, being different is hard, but it can be wonderful, too!" Uncle Maxwell said. "Look at me! Look at Moshe!"

He pointed to a framed black-and-white photograph of Moshe, his great-grandfather and Benny's great-great-grandfather. During every fiddle lesson he included a story about Moshe. Uncle Maxwell rested his hands across his ample belly, cleared his throat, and began:

"On Moshe's ninth birthday, his father, a klezmer

fiddler himself, gave him a violin. It was nothing special—an old, beat-up squawk box of an instrument he bought for next to nothing from a peddler. But when Moshe removed the fiddle from its case, you would have thought his father had given him the finest Stradivarius ever made.

"From the first day, Moshe took to the fiddle like he was born to play it. He practiced day and night, night and day. While other children in the shtetl—the village—played games in the fields, he played *freylekhs* and mazurkas. They called him *tshudne*. That's Yiddish for 'weird.' He could not have cared less.

"'Moshe, play hide and seek with us,' they'd say.

"'No, thanks,' he'd reply. 'I've found what I've been looking for.'"

Benny placed the fiddle under his left jaw line, where a brown mark had formed from many hours of practice. "Can we skip right to the dessert? I learned a new tune from a record I bought yesterday."

"I guess we can bend the rules a bit."

He began "Tantz, Tantz Yiddelech" with a long sliding note, a glissando. The fiddle moaned and wailed. Improvised trills transformed the instrument into a songbird, warbling at his command. The music galloped faster and faster until its melody transported Benny to a faraway place he knew only from his uncle's stories. His bow became a blur of walnut and rosin dust. His frantic fingers raced down a path that stretched deep into the past.

Benny felt invincible. Untouchable. Alive.

When the tune ended, Uncle Maxwell nodded his approval.

For the first time since signing up for the talent show, Benny smiled. A genuine ear-to-ear smile.

Tomorrow meant a return to school.

But for now, there was music.

And that was enough.

♪ **6** ♪

Two yellow buses in front of Sieberling School awaited the sixth-grade classes. *Field trip!* Benny thought. He had forgotten all about going to the Geary Potato Chip Factory. *A perfect distraction. Maybe today won't be so bad.*

A text from Ollie changed his optimism to dread.

Sorry, bro. Sick today. Get some BBQ chips for me.

Benny panicked. With Ollie a no-show he imagined the bus ride could turn into a disaster. At best he would share a seat with someone like himself who just wanted to make it through the day. At worst it meant sitting near You-Know-Who.

In homeroom, students swapped legends about past trips to the factory. Amanda claimed a student fell into a vat of dill-flavored sour cream powder last year and had to be rescued with a crane. Another student swore his cousin stumbled upon the factory's underground potato mine "filled with spuds as big as human heads."

Jason said he had heard that three students had passed

out at the mere whiff of the Terrifying Tater, Geary's hottest chip. He boasted he could eat a bag of them in under five minutes.

Benny remained silent, thankful that salty snack food—and not he—was the morning's chosen topic.

As the lines formed to board the buses, Benny held back. When Jason rushed to the front of the line for the first bus, he darted to the second bus and climbed in.

Walking to the back, Benny slid into a vacant spot and took the window seat. He laid his scarf on the empty space next to him to make it appear occupied. He no sooner had gotten comfortable when he heard a girl's voice. "Is this seat taken?"

"Yes ... I mean ... no," Benny stammered, wrapping the scarf around his neck.

The girl stood almost as tall as Benny, actually taller if you counted the pompom bobbing atop her knit cap. Silver earrings shaped like G-clefs jangled as she plopped down. A hint of jazz leaked from her earbuds.

"Hi! I'm Jennifer. Jennifer Kominsky. I'm in Mr. Browning's class. Call me J-Kom." She wore red horn-rimmed glasses. Short auburn hair peeked out from under her cap and a mouthful of braces flashed when she smiled.

"I'm Benny Feldman. I'm in Ms. Krumholtz's class. Call me ... Benny."

"I moved here a couple of weeks ago. I'm still getting used to the school," Jennifer said.

"So am I," Benny replied. "And I've been here forever."

Be cool, Benny thought. *No need to get too excited. She's new here. That's good. Doesn't know me as the Amazing Exploding Grape. Don't say anything embarrassing, but don't ignore her. Remember rule number one for talking with a new person: Proceed with extreme caution.*

Benny recognized the music coming from Jennifer's phone but said nothing. Jennifer seemed content banging two pencils on her notebook in sync to the music. Sometimes she hit one of the pencils on the metal crossbar in front of her, while using the other to tap out a counter rhythm on the notebook. Her right foot pumped up and down as if working a bass drum pedal. She ended with a fast roll and a cymbal crash, accidently striking the head of the student in front of her.

We're almost there. It's now or never.

"Dave Brubeck Quartet?" Benny asked.

"What?" Jennifer said, taking out an earbud.

"Dave Brubeck Quartet, 'Blue Rondo à la Turk?' Isn't that what you're listening to?"

Jennifer looked more closely at the boy with the thick glasses who nervously tugged at the end of his scarf.

"Yes! How did you know that?"

"My uncle cranks it up when I'm over at his apartment. He has a huge music collection. The rondo starts in nine-eight time and shifts to four-four. I could see you playing along."

"It's from an album my father plays a lot. He's a jazz drummer. I take lessons from him."

The bus jarred to a halt. Benny quickly added a new law on how to navigate school: Always take the window seat in the back.

"Coming? The potato chips are calling," Jennifer said. "Mind if I call you B-Man?"

"Yeah, sure, J-Kom," Benny croaked, scrambling down the aisle behind her. He had more to tell her. More to ask her. But it would have to wait.

Walking side by side, J-Kom and B-Man joined the factory tour.

♪

Benny and Jennifer sat together in the last row of the Evelyn A. Geary Memorial Auditorium. From the stage, the company's mascot—a potato wearing a ten-gallon hat and spurred cowboy boots—introduced a short film about the history of the potato chip. Plastered to his rigid foam head was a crooked, frozen grin that seemed to say, "There's got to be a better way to make a living."

"Howdy, pardners! I'm Chip! The rootinest, tootinest root vegetable this side of the Boise River," he said in a fake Western drawl. The pre-recorded words came from speakers mounted on the walls. Chip clutched a basket brimming with real potatoes against his red flannel shirt.

Benny couldn't look at him. *Stage. Bad costume. Hot lights.*

Jason lurking nearby. He focused instead on the G-clefs hanging from Jennifer's ears.

The auditorium lights dimmed and the film began, but Benny wasn't interested in how many pounds of potato chips were consumed every year. Music was on his mind. He plotted his next move: *Start discussing jazz, then slip in a reference to klezmer.*

"What do you think of Nina Simone, Miles Davis, Django Reinhardt?" Benny asked. *Bless you, Uncle Maxwell, for playing their records.*

"Love them all!" Jennifer said. "Jazz is always on at our house. What music do you like?"

The question set off fireworks in Benny's mind. His brain downloaded at least a gigabyte's worth of music he had absorbed during his lessons. He breathlessly poured out a mishmash of musicians and genres, from acid rock to bluegrass, classical to soul. Talking at the speed of an auctioneer, he started with guitarist Jimi Hendrix and ended with cellist Yo-Yo Ma, making sure to mention his interest in Aboriginal didgeridoo music, barbershop quartets, and the Beatles in between.

"A great mix," Jennifer said.

"Uncle Maxwell says all music is connected … and music connects us all."

Ms. Krumholtz broke in before Benny could mention his klezmer favorites. "Shh," she said. "I suggest taking notes. There will be a quiz on this later."

The film credits scrolled and Chip reappeared. A

student tossed a wadded-up brochure at the mascot's gaping mouth as if trying to score a three-pointer in corn hole. It glanced off the potato's forehead and bounced across the floor. A low, communal "boooooo" rose from the audience.

"I appreciate ya bein' such fine guests," the pre-recorded tape said as a paper airplane lodged squarely in the mascot's right eye. "Now's the time for the ol' Chipster to mosey off into the sunset. Y'all have a crunch-tastic time during ya visit, ya hear."

A company guide led the sixth-graders on the rest of the tour: the washing and peeling machine, whirring conveyor belts, the cavernous warehouse where bags were stored, another room filled with boxes for packing and shipping the chips all over Ohio, and towering white tubs holding ingredients "I'm not allowed to divulge, so let's move along," the guide said.

Benny and Jennifer were inseparable on the tour. The pair discovered they enjoyed old arcade games; were not fond of Mr. Mettner, their gym teacher; knew all the lyrics to *The Brady Bunch* theme; and preferred mild chips over scorching hot. Benny had never met anyone—a girl, no less—so easy to talk to, so interested in what he had to say. And who laughed so loudly at her own corny jokes.

"What did the drummer drink for breakfast?" she asked.

"No idea."

"Beat juice."

Benny concluded that "proceed with extreme caution" did not apply when a drummer and possible klezmer band member accompanied you to a potato chip factory. Halfway through the tour, Benny made a decision: He would tell Jennifer about his fiddling and ask her to join the band on the ride back to school.

The tour's final stop was the tasting room, where students could sample "All fifteen fabulous flavors of Geary Potato Chips!" as the guide explained. Scanning the room for Jason, Benny craned his neck—a bespectacled periscope searching for enemy crafts in dangerous waters. He was nowhere in sight.

This has been the best day of school ever! Benny thought. He corrected himself. *No, this has been the best day of my life!*

Across the room a crowd gathered around a display of the Terrifying Tater. According to Geary's official heat scale, this chip ranked a ten out of ten. Its bag showed a cartoon rendering of Chip with plumes of smoke billowing from his mouth and ears.

A growing chant of "Go! Go! Go! Go! Go!" arose from the crowd. It parted to reveal Jason shoveling handfuls of the jalapeno and cayenne pepper chips into his mouth like a raccoon raiding a trash can.

"Three minutes, fifteen seconds!" whooped a student who was timing Jason.

Jason held up the last chip between red-stained fingers and walked toward Benny. His cheering section followed.

Please. Not now. Not today.

"I saved this one for you," Jason said, belching spicy fumes. "You're not scared of a little-bitty chip? Afraid it might make you *EXPLODE*?"

Benny briefly considered popping the chip into his mouth and chewing it slowly with a satisfied grin. This was impossible. As a preschooler, he had mistakenly doused Grandma Feldman's meatloaf in extra-hot sauce rather than ketchup and ended up in bed clutching his stomach.

So Benny did nothing.

"Ha! I knew you couldn't do it!" Jason said.

Benny tried to think of a comeback, a devastating retort that would send this long-haired Neanderthal skulking back to his cave.

"How can you get on stage with your band if you can't face a teeny-widdle chip?" Jason crushed it in his hand and let the pieces fall to the floor.

"I-I- ...." Benny stuttered.

"I bet you don't even *have* a band. In fact, I'm *positive* you don't have a band. Come on, Feldman, who's in your All-Star Klezmer Band?"

"I am. I'm the drummer," Jennifer said, walking through the crowd and standing beside Benny. "Let's go, B-Man. The bus is waiting." She and Benny brushed past Jason.

Benny turned around before reaching the door. "And I'm the fiddler," he said. "Any more questions?"

♪

On the ride back to school, Benny filled in Jennifer on what just happened in the potato chip factory. He had only met her that morning but trusted her in a way he could not explain. No one, except Ollie, had ever stood up for him like she had.

Words spilled out about the Sabbath play, Jason, his fiddling, his love of klezmer, and the imaginary band written in black marker on the talent show sign-up sheet.

Suddenly, Amanda stuck her head between them from the seat behind. "101,002 views," she said, shoving her phone in Benny's face before leaning back.

"What was *that* all about?" Jennifer asked.

"Another piece of the story," Benny said.

Benny borrowed Jennifer's phone and found a tune by the Klezmatics, one of his favorite bands.

"It's called 'Rebns Khasene/Khasene Tants.' That's Yiddish for 'The Rabbi's Wedding' and 'Wedding Dance.' *This* is klezmer," he said, handing her the phone.

Benny watched Jennifer's expression as she listened, expecting to see her smile change to a grimace. Instead, she took two pencils from her notebook and began to improvise drum fills as the music shifted from mournful to buoyant.

"Well?" Benny asked.

"Well what?"

Benny's heart sank. *She hated it. Not cool enough. Why*

would she want to be in my band anyway? I'm probably going to end up like Chip someday.

"It totally kicks, B-Man! A real challenge, too. Who wouldn't like this?"

Now the moment of truth. "So what you told Jason—that was for real?"

"Why did the chicken join the band?" Jennifer asked.

"Don't know."

"Because they needed a couple of drumsticks."

≳ ♪ ≲

Searching for Hanukkah wrapping paper, Benny trailed his mother through the maze of giant candy canes and animatronic elves decorating the mall gift shop. At the end of an aisle, beside strands of blinking snowmen and Christmas lights, they discovered a hidden cove of wooden dreidels, bags of gelt, and a few shiny rolls not covered with sleigh-pulling reindeer or jolly St. Nicks.

"Should we go with the Stars of David or the menorahs this year?" Mrs. Feldman asked. She held a plastic-wrapped cylinder in each hand.

After his day at the potato chip factory, Benny didn't care if the wrapping paper was red and green and covered with ornament-filled evergreen trees. Ignoring his mother's holiday dilemma, he texted Ollie.

How r u feeling?

Better. How was potato-land?

Got a bag of BBQs for you.

Thx!

Btw, the band has a drummer.

What band?

The klezmer band.

Right. Who is he?

HER name is Jennifer Kominsky.

She's in my class. Tall. Bangs pencils on her desk.

That's her!

So this is happening?

We'll see.

Mrs. Feldman tapped Benny on the shoulder. "Earth to Benny. A little distracted, are we?"

You have no idea. G-clef earrings, Dave Brubeck, the Chipster, and Jason's shocked expression danced in his mind.

"I've decided to play in the talent show," Benny said, focusing on the three available designs of Hanukkah cards.

Outwardly, Mrs. Feldman remained composed. Inside she was *kvelling*—bursting with pride. This was not a run-of-the-mill *kvell*, but a pressure-cooker-about-to-blow-its-top *kvell*. The Krakatoa of *kvells*!

"So, how did this come about?" she asked.

"I found a drummer."

"Who is he?"

"HER name is Jennifer Kominsky."

Benny watched his mother process the news. He could

read the thought bubble above her head: *My son will be leading a band. Performing on stage. With a girl drummer— a girl he must have actually talked to!*

Benny feared his mother might spontaneously combust.

"I can't wait to tell Aunt Esther and Uncle Fred, and your cousins Sara and…."

"Please don't make a big deal of it, Mom. I still need to find a clarinet player and an accordionist. It might not happen."

A bit of joy leaked from his mother like a Macy's Thanksgiving balloon dropping a little closer to the parade below.

"You can do it," she said. "Keep trying."

Benny glanced at another text from Ollie.

Finished your personal essay?

Arghh! Haven't started.

Due on Thursday. No extensions! LOL.

Frisbee at the park tomorrow?

You bet! Bring the chips!

♪ 7 ♪

After school, Benny and Ollie walked to Ardmore City Park. They always played frisbee in the middle of a field at the south end. Benny insisted on this spot, far away from the basketball courts.

Benny looked forward to this weekly ritual as much as he did his violin lessons. The boys counted out loud the number of consecutive catches made without the disc touching the ground: "Thirty-five … thirty-six … thirty-seven … thirty-eight…." If they reached 100 throws without a miss, they would celebrate by stopping by Marconi's Nut Stand for a bag of cashews. That was the deal. One drop, no nuts.

They had made it to ninety-six when a group of teenagers throwing a football stormed the field.

"You'll have to move unless you want to get run over," one of them demanded. "This is our field now."

"No problem," Ollie replied. "We'll go over there." He pointed to the field next to the basketball courts.

Benny's face paled. "Let's go home. I should be working on my essay."

"You've got lots of time. We've only been here for half an hour. C'mon, just a few more tosses."

"No! I have to leave now!"

"What's wrong?"

Benny viewed the empty basketball courts. In his mind he saw classmates fighting for rebounds. He heard the sounds of leather hitting pavement, loud cheering, and then ringing laughter. Ollie watched Benny staring blankly at the courts.

"I don't want to talk about it," Benny said, turning.

"Does it have something to do with basketball? Help me out here." Ollie was asking questions again, and Benny didn't like it one bit.

"No," he said, walking faster.

Ollie stopped as Benny charged well ahead. "I can't help if you don't tell me! That's what best friends do!"

Benny let Ollie catch up. It was no use. Ollie wasn't going to let this go. So Benny told him why Jason was still teasing him after all these years.

♪

Benny dreaded going to the fifth-grade picnic at Ardmore City Park. Every spring fifth-graders from Sieberling School were joined by their rivals from Old Harbor Academy. For decades, the two schools had competed against each other in a series of events: a tug of war, potato-sack race, egg drop, water balloon throw, and 100-yard dash.

The final matchup was a five-on-five basketball game. The rules were simple—the first team to score ten baskets would be declared the winner.

Benny managed to avoid being picked for any of the competitions. He was happy roaming the sidelines as the schools battled for the most points.

By mid-afternoon, Sieberling and Old Harbor were tied. The team that won the basketball game would snatch the trophy.

As the Sieberling team captain, Jason started picking the best basketball players from his school. The Old Harbor captain did likewise. Everyone's jaws dropped when Old Harbor's secret weapon appeared. Arriving late to the picnic was a foreign exchange student from Belgium named Leopold. He stood a head taller than anyone there, except for one. Leopold spun the ball on his index finger and casually sent a perfect shot into the net.

Jason knew there was only one Sieberling student who could match Leopold's height and arm span. That student's curly head poked above the crowd of onlookers. Benny gulped hard and ducked as Jason stared in his direction.

Jason won't pick me. Not a chance. No way.

"Get up here, Feldman," Jason said flatly. "You're in."

Benny tried to turn and run, but his classmates pushed him onto the court. It was all happening too fast.

"Let's win this for Sieberling," Jason urged, giving each player instructions. Then he faced Benny.

"Okay, Feldman. All you have to do is stay in front of the tall guy. That's it. Don't let him out of your sight. Keep your arms straight up. And no shooting. If the ball comes to you, pass it to me—fast! Got it?"

Benny gulped again and nodded.

The whistle blew and bodies flew in every direction. Benny's head jerked from side to side as the ball zipped around the court. Taking long strides, he followed Old Harbor's giant center up and down the court until his lungs ached. When Leopold took his first shot—a ten-footer from the corner—Benny stretched his arms as high as he could and extended his fingers. To everyone's amazement, the ball deflected off his right hand and landed in front of Jason, who dribbled down the court and made the first basket.

Every time Leopold took a shot, Benny was there—a long-armed shadow running on pure adrenaline and fear. Sweat poured into Benny's eyes, but he was sure he saw Jason give him a grin and a thumbs-up.

With the score tied nine to nine, Old Harbor's captain tried to bank in a long hook shot. It bounced off the backboard and right into Benny's hands. Stunned, he looked down at the orb as if it was a crystal ball that could tell him what to do next. As his opponents charged, Benny held the ball above his head and spied Jason underneath the basket.

He remembered Jason's instructions: *Pass it to me—fast!*

So Benny did. He hurled the ball downward, startling Jason by the force of the throw. It struck him squarely on the top of his head and bounded upward. Jason fell backward and hit the ground hard. The ball hung on the rim for an agonizing second before dropping through the net with a gentle swish.

With an assist from Jason's cranium, Benny had made the winning basket—for the Old Harbor team.

Laughter filled the park. Dazed from the blow, Jason lay on his back and listened to the stream of comments:

"Way to use your head, Conroy!"

"Look, it's LeBrain James!"

"Hey, I thought soccer season was over!"

Benny said nothing. Instead, he flashed back to the Sabbath play and Jason rocking on his back in a challah costume. He knew what would happen tomorrow at school. Jason would call him the Amazing Exploding Grape again. And the day after that … and the day after that … and the day after that….

♪

"So that's the whole story between Jason and me," Benny said. "I not only lost the game, but I embarrassed him—

for the second time. After that, things at school went from so-so to just plain awful."

"How awful?" Ollie asked.

"In homeroom the next day, Jason made sure everyone knew I lost the game for Sieberling. He made sure everyone knew I was no longer Benny Feldman. I was the Amazing—you know. Jason is popular. People follow him."

"Like sheep."

"Like sheep," Benny repeated.

"So why didn't you tell me about this?"

Benny blushed. "I was embarrassed, too. Still am. I'm tired of messing up everything."

"Why *that* nickname?"

"I guess some things don't completely go away."

"Anything I can do?" Ollie asked.

"Yeah, learn the clarinet!"

"Sorry, I'm an artist, not a musician," he said, handing Benny a barbeque potato chip as they walked home.

♫ **8** ♫

Benny had put off writing the essay which had been assigned to all the sixth-grade classes. The topic was "A Person I Admire." The problem was deciding on a subject. He considered his mother, a public defender who represented people who could not afford a lawyer. He also thought about selecting his father, a newspaper editor who believed in the power of the written word and printing the truth. How could he pick one over the other? Then there was Uncle Maxwell, who had introduced him to klezmer.

Outside of his family, Benny weighed Bob Dylan against Bob Marley. Itzhak Perlman versus the Dixie Chicks. Beethoven beside Aaron Copland. None seemed the perfect choice.

Ms. Krumholtz had warned the class that it was unacceptable—under any circumstances—to write the essay about her, as one student did every year. "While I appreciate the thought, I wasn't born yesterday. Doing so will not guarantee you an automatic A."

After practicing his violin, a light clicked on inside Benny's head. He decided to write his essay about his great-great-grandfather Moshe.

≳ ♫ ≲

Unlike most of his classmates, Benny declined the option of reading his essay aloud. Looking at the list on the blackboard, he noticed Jason had signed up to read.

Of course he would. Another chance to show off. He probably wrote about some guitar hero.

Amanda went first.

"My essay is about PSY, the South Korean rapper whose video, 'Gangnam Style,' was the first video on YouTube to reach one billion views. This is slightly more than my baton-twirling video, but can PSY do this?"

She cartwheeled across the front of the classroom, knocking a stapler and tape dispenser off Ms. Krumholtz's desk. Then she did a split and flung a baton toward the ceiling. It bounced off a light fixture and landed in her outstretched right hand.

The class cheered. "Thank you, Amanda. That was ... uh ... very interesting," Ms. Krumholtz said.

How is Jason going to follow that performance? Benny thought as he watched his nemesis shuffle to the front of the class. He noticed Jason's subdued expression and the slight slouch of his shoulders.

Jason brushed his blond hair out of his eyes. "My essay is titled, 'My Dad.'"

"My dad, Aaron Conroy, is an Air Force captain. He told me that ever since he was a boy, he dreamed of soaring in the sky like an eagle. As a pilot, he flies an F-15 Eagle jet, so I guess you could say his dream came true. Flying a fighter plane is dangerous. My mom and I worry about him all the time. Sometimes I wish he drove a truck around town instead. That way he could be closer to the ground and closer to home. But we know he has a really important job, and he always says a clear blue sky is a lot safer than a busy freeway.

"Being in the Air Force means Dad is away from the family in far-off countries fighting for our freedom, even during holidays like Thanksgiving and Hanukkah, or when I'm pitching in Little League, or playing with my band at the talent show. He Skypes with us, but it's not the same as when he's home working on his Mustang, wrestling with our wiener dog, watching football with me, or dancing the twist with my mom in the living room.

"The best time I have with my dad is when he gives me guitar lessons. He says I'm a heck of a fine picker who can make my ax sing, which means I'm darn good.

"Someday I hope to be as good as him. He's my hero."

Benny watched Jason return to his seat and put his hands over his face. He could not imagine spending holidays without his father or not seeing him at the dinner table every night. Benny tried to think of the right words to say, but Jason spoke first.

"One lousy fiddle and some drums. That's all you've got? The Neanderthal Four are going to steamroll right over you."

So much for feeling sorry for Jason. He doesn't make it easy.

≩ ♪ ≨

Benny's essay lay on his nightstand. Across the top Ms. Krumholtz had written: "I wish you had shared Moshe's story with the class. A+"

Staring at the stapled sheets, Benny felt as if he had let down the entire family: his great-great-grandfather, great-grandfather, grandfather, uncle, and all the klezmer musicians who came before them.

Maybe the class would understand me a little better if I'd read it? Fat chance. They'd have asked if Moshe had ever exploded when he played.

Picking up the essay, Benny read it before his reflection in the mirror:

"During my violin lessons, my Uncle Maxwell tells me stories about Moshe, my great-great-grandfather. He was a klezmer fiddler like me, tall with long, thin fingers, and one of the best fiddlers in all of Russia.

"Moshe was born in 1865. Like many klezmer musicians back then, he earned a living traveling from town to town. His home was wherever he fiddled.

"One night, Moshe would be playing a Jewish wedding in Odessa, the next night a private party in Bilyaivka, and then a solo performance in the market square in Zatoka. Other klezmer musicians joined him—accordionists, clarinetists, cellists, trombonists, and drummers. He would jam with anyone who loved music as much as he did. What made him so good? Moshe played every note like his life depended on it.

"Being a klezmer fiddler wasn't easy. Sometimes his bands played non-stop for hours while people drank and danced. A wedding could last an entire day. Once a man threw a bottle and knocked him out. Another time the local police broke up a party and ran the band out of town.

"Moshe's fingers ached. His back hurt from standing. Sometimes, after fiddling his heart out, he didn't get paid. But he always said, 'Things could be worse.'

"Uncle Maxwell says klezmer is part of my DNA because Moshe came from a family of klezmer musicians dating back to the 1500s. Some of the tunes he played were from Romanian and Ukrainian folk songs. Others were from ancient melodies cantors in synagogues chanted a cappella—that means singing without instruments. When I hear the sad melodies during Yom Kippur services, I fiddle along in my mind. It makes me feel like I'm part of something special, a part of something beautiful.

"The tradition of playing klezmer was passed down to

my Uncle Maxwell, who taught me to play. I am who I am because of those who came before me, like Moshe."

Benny ran his fingers across the top of the page. *I wish you had shared Moshe's story.* He made himself a promise that next time he would.

♪ 9 ♪

Benny, Jennifer, and Ollie surveyed the school cafeteria, hoping to recruit more band members. Benny remained realistic. He didn't have high expectations of anyone pulling out an accordion and playing a bouncy version of "Bublitschki" over mushy mashed potatoes and half-eaten slabs of Salisbury steak.

Word had spread about the klezmer band, but few students were begging to enlist. A third-grader in Sunday school offered to play the kazoo. A fifth-grader auditioned at recess by attempting "Yankee Doodle" on the recorder. Amanda said she would hold a bucket in case Benny lost his dinner during the show.

"How about Paul Grouper? Doesn't he play the clarinet?" Jennifer asked.

"No go. He's good buddies with Jason. Besides, he ditched the clarinet for football," Benny said.

"There's Cynthia Redfern. I *know* she plays the clarinet in the band," Jennifer suggested.

"She's a definite no. Once she had an allergic reaction to the pickled herring I brought for lunch. She won't get anywhere near me now."

Jennifer and Benny went back and forth discussing potential band members and klezmer tunes. This went on for most of the lunch period. Ollie tried to make a comment, but there was no stopping Benny's single-minded focus.

"Can we talk about something other than klezmer for once?!" Ollie pleaded.

"I've got it!" Benny said. "Fred Bradford. He plays the oboe, but maybe he can switch over."

"Maybe," Ollie sighed.

Benny got up to leave. "I volunteered to sort cans for the winter food drive. Anyone want to join me?"

"Catch you later," Ollie said. "I'm still eating."

"I'll help," Jennifer said.

≳ ♪ ≲

In the storage room behind the stage, stacks of creamed corn and lima beans ran neck and neck for the most-donated foods. Sliced beets and succotash were a close second. Cans of soup lay scattered on the floor like escapees from a Warhol painting. By the door sat a Black Panther backpack, a small instrument case, and pages of sheet music.

"Hey, I'm Royce Jenkins," said a seventh-grader

emerging from behind a jumble of empty boxes. Benny had passed by Royce many times in the hallway. His preferred attire—a loud bow tie and a white button-down shirt covered with a superhero T-shirt—made him hard to miss. Benny also recognized him as the school's spelling bee champion three years running.

"Hi, I'm Benny."

"Jennifer—call me J-Kom."

"You in trouble, too?" Royce asked.

"No, we volunteered," Benny said.

"Well, I was sent here by the band teacher. I'm a clarinet player without a home."

Benny and Jennifer exchanged a did-he-just-say-clarinet look.

"What did you do?" Jennifer asked.

"The band was playing 'Let It Snow' for the five millionth time using the same boring arrangement we do every year. I couldn't take it anymore."

"So what happened?" Benny asked.

"I jazzed it up a bit—gave it a little more holiday spirit. Mr. Coffin wasn't happy so he sent me here. He can be a C-U-R-M-U-D-G-E-O-N when I break from the page."

"Break from the page?" Jennifer asked.

"It means do my own thing. Take the music in a cosmic direction."

"Could you show us?" Benny asked.

Royce took out his clarinet, wet the reed with his lips, and, like a snake charmer, coaxed hypnotic sounds out of the ebony instrument. He started playing "Let It Snow" like they did in band, steady and familiar. He slowly added a dusting of notes to the melody, then a flurry, and finally a blizzard of improvisation that changed the tune into something totally different and crazy. After playing for several minutes, he returned to the original melody—for the five million and first time.

While Royce played, Jennifer banged pencils on fruit cocktail cans and Benny bowed an "air fiddle" to the music. When Royce finished, Benny expected the cans of garbanzo beans and baby peas to burst into applause.

"That was fantastic!" Jennifer said.

"Amazing!" Benny agreed. "What do you play other than jazz?"

"I accompany my church's gospel choir with my mother. She's a flutist, the first African-American in the Ardmore Symphony's woodwind section. But my true passion is classical." He handed Benny the sheet music for Mozart's Clarinet Concerto in A Major.

Benny smiled. "Classical, huh? Do you know the beginning of Gershwin's *Rhapsody in Blue*?"

Without a word, Royce trilled on a low G. He rapidly climbed seventeen notes, sliding up to a high C like an express elevator going from the lobby to the top floor of a skyscraper in three seconds. Benny knew it as the most famous klezmer glissando ever written.

Proceed with extreme caution? Not when there's a clarinet prodigy standing right in front of me.

Benny seized the moment. "We're putting together a klezmer band for the talent show. Would you like to join us?"

"That's Jewish music, right?" Royce said. "The band plays 'I Have a Little Dreidel' every year at the winter concert. Last spring I was part of the orchestra when the drama department put on 'Fiddler on the Roof.'"

"That's a start," Jennifer said. "You can ask Benny anything. He's a walking encyclopedia on the subject."

"Klezmer goes way back," Benny said. "Long ago the word 'klezmer' just meant 'musical instrument.' Then it referred to the musicians themselves. Now the word means the type of music our band will play."

"Klezmer cooks," Jennifer added.

"No more 'Let It Snow'?"

"Nope. That's a promise," Benny said.

"I'll R-U-M-I-N-A-T-E on it."

"Definition?" Benny asked.

"Ruminate. A verb meaning to chew on. To ponder."

"So you'll think about it?" Jennifer said.

"Yes. Meanwhile, hand me those cans of kidney beans."

♩ ♪ ♩

The next day Benny and Jennifer found Royce back in the storage room, sorting boxes of instant rice and angel-hair pasta.

"Hey! It's J-Kom and Benny. Come join me. Lots of new stock today—pear slices, lentil soup, pineapple chunks, and asparagus spears."

"Did you get in trouble again?" Benny asked.

"No, I volunteered. Mr. Coffin didn't mind me leaving the clarinet section for the day. I think he was afraid of what I might do to 'Winter Wonderland.' And it was fun hanging out with you guys."

"So?" Jennifer said, tugging the snare drum earrings she wore for good luck.

"Ah, the klezmer band."

Jennifer shot him a what-else-would-I-be-talking-about look.

"I listened to a lot of klezmer tunes last night," Royce said. "The clarinet playing is insane!" He reeled off a list of names Benny knew as well as the cracks in his bedroom ceiling.

"There's Giora Feidman, Margot Leverett, Don Byron, and that's just the beginning," Royce said.

"Have a favorite?" Benny asked.

"Too hard to choose. Some musicians are traditional. I heard hip-hop, electronic music, jazz, even some players banging kitchen utensils. White, black, Latino...."

"It's all over the map," Benny said.

"Yep. My mother says music is about bringing people together," Royce said.

"She sounds like my Uncle Maxwell."

"So are you in?" Jennifer asked.

"Yes, I'll join your band. If I'm going to be a professional clarinetist, I better know how to play klezmer. But I have a few conditions." He readjusted the blue bow tie above his Ant Man T-shirt.

"What kind of conditions?" Benny asked.

"First, I need time to study for the local spelling bee. It happens around the same time as the talent show. Second, it's going to take some practice to learn klezmer clarinet in such a short time. I'm not sure I can pull it off. If I decide I'm not ready, I want the right to pull out of the band."

"I can live with that," Benny said.

"One last thing. I've never heard either of you play. I won't join if you're no good. Are you any good?"

A fair question. I've only played for Uncle Maxwell. Jennifer has never heard me, and I haven't really heard her drum except on a notebook and some tin cans. I'm not sure any of us can pull this off. What if the talent show turns into the first-grade play all over again?

Jennifer jumped in. "Benny is by far the best klezmer fiddler in Sieberling School."

You mean the only one, Benny laughed to himself.

"You'll have to trust us. We're going to be something special," Jennifer said.

Royce reached out and gave Benny and Jennifer a firm handshake. "Let's go for it."

"Great," Benny said. He tried to remain calm. *Just some musicians forming a band. No big deal. Happens every day.*

Inside, Benny was shouting as if he'd won the lottery. He felt like climbing the tower of stewed tomatoes, beating his chest and shouting, "I, Benny Feldman, am King Kong of the klezmer world!"

"With your help, we'll destroy Jason," Jennifer said.

"Who's Jason?" Royce asked. "And why do we have to *destroy* him?"

"Oh, he plays in the Neanderthal Four. That's the band that won the talent show last year," Benny said.

"You didn't tell me this was a competition," Royce said, frowning.

"The top three acts win trophies," Benny said.

"Music isn't a battle between Spiderman and Doc Ock. And it's not about winning trophies. When you do it right, everyone wins."

"I know, but wait until you meet Jason," Jennifer said.

"By the way, do you know any accordion players?" Benny asked.

Royce scrunched up his face. "Accordion, no. But I'll keep my ears open."

♪

On his way to math class, Benny flashed back to the days after the Sabbath play. He had hoped the whole incident would blow over like a fast-moving storm. His parents had convinced him everything would be fine at school.

They were wrong.

In the hallway, Benny saw classmates gathered around Jason, teasing him about toppling on stage. Everyone laughed as one student rocked back and forth on the floor. Benny could tell Jason had been crying.

Amanda wobbled next to Benny's desk and pretended to throw up. For the first time, Benny heard Jason call him the Amazing Exploding Grape.

It was worse at Sunday school. Karen, the Grossman twins, and Jason were all mocked until Mrs. Mandelbaum told everyone to stop. Eventually, Benny became the focus—the boy in the grape costume who brought their play to a crashing halt. Benny tried to say he was sorry for what happened.

"It was an accident. I had a bad cold. My brother said it was the best Sabbath play ever."

They ignored him. Soon the play faded from almost everyone's memory.

Nobody had called Benny the Amazing Exploding Grape for years. But now, thanks to Jason and one unlucky bounce of a basketball, it was stuck to him again like glue. He wondered what names would stick to Royce and Jennifer if he blundered at the talent show.

♪ 10 ♪

On the first night of Hanukkah, the smell of fried potato latkes wafted through the Feldman house. Upstairs, Benny wrapped the slightly lopsided menorah he had made in art class. With Ollie's help, it looked a little more like a piece of modern art and a little less like a multi-armed mollusk. Across the hall Sam practiced his post-holiday-dinner juggling routine. He tossed wooden dreidels into the air while singing loudly and out of tune:

> I have a little dreidel,
> I made it out of clay,
> And when it's dry and ready,
> Oh dreidel I will play.

Sam's holiday yodeling usually drove Benny nuts, but something felt different about Hanukkah this year. Benny had a klezmer band—at least three-fourths of one. He picked up his fiddle and played along until his uncle showed up.

♪

Uncle Maxwell arrived with his ukulele under his arm and gifts wrapped in the Sunday comics section.

"Max, you outdid yourself this year," Mrs. Feldman said, giving her brother a hug. "Which store sold you this wrapping paper?"

"Ha ha. Do you have any idea how many weeks' worth of newspapers this represents? Besides, this gives you a chance to catch up on Garfield."

Uncle Maxwell put his ukulele on the piano bench. Every year, after the Hanukkah dinner, he performed a Jewish parody song and passed out lyric sheets so everyone could sing along. Last year he sang two songs by the famous jazz clarinetist Mickey Katz: "How Much Is That Pickle in the Window?" and "Borscht Riders in the Sky." Benny didn't understand all the inside jokes and Yiddish words, but he enjoyed seeing his uncle and parents doubled over with laughter.

Benny's job was to light the first candle. Standing together, the family recited the Hanukkah prayers as he used the shamash to ignite the single candle on the far right of the menorah. The twin flames filled the room with a warm glow.

"Come and get 'em before I eat all the latkes!" Mr.

Feldman shouted. He flung open the French doors to the dining room.

Uncle Maxwell's passion for music was equaled only by his love of food. He devoured a big stack of potato pancakes, two helpings of brisket slow-cooked to tangy perfection, and a hefty slice of heavenly angel food cake. Stretching, he pushed himself away from the table.

"Delicious," he said. "I guess I can forgive you for the wrapping paper comments. Now let's open some gifts."

While some Jewish families doled out one gift for each night of Hanukkah, Feldman family tradition called for opening all the presents on the first night. This suited Benny and Sam. Their Sunday school classmates said that by the final night, the gifts dwindled to pairs of sports socks and packages of tighty whities. As their father said, "Life's too short to wait."

Benny held up a gift covered in Family Circus and Dilbert characters. "Hmmm, I bet this one is from … Uncle Maxwell!"

"Okay, smart guy, let's see what you got."

Inside was a framed photograph of Moshe.

"For inspiration. Oh, and one more thing." Uncle Maxwell removed his brown fedora and placed it on Benny's head. "A klezmer musician isn't fully dressed without a snazzy hat."

"Thanks! I love it!"

Benny's parents gave him a group pass to the upcoming comic book and arcade show at the Ardmore

Convention Center. Practically every kid in town attended the annual event. Some came dressed as superheroes, animé characters, sci-fi icons, and mutants of their own creation. Comic book artists and television celebrities would be there signing autographs. Benny had heard that the main hall would be filled with rows of pinball machines and vintage arcade games like Space Invaders, Galaga, Asteroids, Centipede, and Donkey Kong.

"Maybe you can take Ollie and your new friends," Mrs. Feldman said. "Here are rolls of quarters for the machines."

"And here's your gift I made in school," Benny said.

"You have the soul of an artist!" his mother said, holding up his menorah.

"Cool! A squid with Hebrew letters!" Sam said.

"It's not a…. Oh, never mind," Benny sighed.

After Sam finished his juggling routine, Uncle Maxwell took out his ukulele. "This year I wrote a song of my own called 'Eight Days a Year.' It's sung to the tune of 'Eight Days a Week' by the Beatles."

As Uncle Maxwell passed out the lyrics, Benny faced his parents. "I've got one more present for you. Just a second." He raced to his room and came back with his violin.

"Maestro," Benny said, gesturing to his uncle with a sweeping motion of his left hand. Uncle Maxwell plucked out the opening notes while Benny fiddled along:

Oy, I need your latkes, yes, you know I do!
And we'll spin the dreidel, sing a song or two.
Buy 'em! Fry 'em! Peel 'em! Feel 'em!
We ain't got nothing but latkes, eight days a year!

Candy canes are alright and so is mistletoe,
But give me a splash of oil and a plump po-ta-to!
Buy 'em! Fry 'em! Peel 'em! Feel 'em!
We ain't got nothing but latkes, eight days a year!

Eight days a year, we light the menorah.
Eight days a year, we sing and dance the hora!

We eat up all the latkes, fat and spherical,
But we still have room for brisket, now that's a
    miracle!
Buy 'em! Fry 'em! Peel 'em! Feel 'em!
We ain't got nothing but latkes, eight days a year!

Eight days a year, we eat with Uncle Saul.
Eight days a year, we forget about cholesterol!

Oy! I need your latkes, yes, you know I do!
And we'll spin the dreidel, sing a song or two.
Buy 'em! Fry 'em! Peel 'em! Feel 'em!
We ain't got nothing but latkes, eight days a year!
Eight days a year! Eight days a year!

Sam led the family dancing around the living room, singing and bumping into each other like dizzy dreidels.

Surrounded by his family, Benny's nervousness about performing disappeared. At the end of the song, he added a few rounds of "Tantz, Tantz Yiddelech."

A small step, but still a long way from being on stage at the talent show, he thought.

This was the first time Benny had ever played for his parents. They had listened to the music from outside his bedroom door, wondering how the happiness or sadness of the tune he played reflected his mood that day. Sometimes it was a mixture of both. This time there was little doubt: What streamed from Benny's fiddle on this first night of Hanukkah was the sound of pure joy.

"The menorah you gave us is lovely," Mrs. Feldman said. "But this … this…." Tears dropped from her eyes as the candles melted into glistening pools of blue wax.

≳ ♪ ≲

Benny hung the photograph of Moshe across from his bed. The weathered fedora rested on his dresser next to the alarm clock.

Looking at his great-great-grandfather, Benny saw a man in his mid-thirties wearing a stern expression. Uncle Maxwell had told him that Jewish families in Russia and Eastern Europe lived in constant fear of being driven from their homes, or worse. Despite this, Moshe was known for having a sense of humor and a big laugh lurking beneath his bushy beard.

"How else could he have survived such uncertain times?" Uncle Maxwell had said. "How else could he have played with such jubilation?"

Recalling his uncle's many stories, Benny spoke to the photo and imagined Moshe's reply:

"So where am I going to find an accordion player?"

Back in my day, you couldn't walk down the street without bumping into two or three accordionists. On Sundays it practically rained accordionists. You've never heard of the Great Accordion Flood of 1888?

Benny's phone jingled. It was a text from Jennifer.

How was H-kah?

Sweet! I've got a surprise for the band. He glanced at the group pass to the convention.

Btw, when's practice?

When we find an accordion player.

Which means ... NEVER!

I used to believe in never, too.

I'm itching to play!!!

Soon, I promise!

♪ 11 ♪

Over the next week Benny racked his brain trying to think of where he might find an accordion player. He concluded that he would have a better chance of discovering a sixth-grader who could sing Italian opera.

During lunch, Jennifer suggested other instruments that might work. "I've watched klezmer bands online that use cellists and trumpeters. There's some that have a piano or a synthesizer. Hey, what about a harmonica?"

Benny remained stubborn on this point. "I'm sorry," he said. "We need an accordion. That's how I want the band to sound."

"What about a tuba?" Jennifer asked.

"Nope."

"A trombone?"

"Nope."

"A mandolin?"

"Don't think so."

Jennifer looked crossly at Benny. "B-Man, are you using this as an excuse for not performing?"

"What do you mean?"

"It seems like if you don't find an accordion player, then we don't have a band. And without a band, you don't have to get on stage at the talent show."

She's right—kind of. I do want an accordion for the sound, though I guess I wouldn't mind if I didn't find one.

"No, that's not it at all," Benny lied.

"Well, it needs to happen soon. The show isn't far away, and Jason's band is miles ahead of us."

"Don't I know it."

♪

That night, Benny received a text from Ollie:

Coming over Saturday? The Monster-Thon is on cable.

No can do.

Why? I'll make popcorn.

I need to practice.

ALL DAY?

Yes, the talent show is coming in a couple of months. I don't want to mess up.

You'll miss all 3 MegaBreath movies!

Sorry. Maybe next time.

Maybe.

Ollie read the string of texts. They looked similar to

the ones he had exchanged with Benny the week before. And the week before that.

≥ ♪ ≤

At Benny's lesson, the memory of his Hanukkah performance lingered in his head. He played each scale and finger exercise with a newfound confidence, pretending he was on stage before a screaming crowd.

"Must be the hat," Uncle Maxwell said. "I believe I saw smoke rising from your fiddle."

For the lesson's klezmer tune, Benny once again chose "Tantz, Tantz Yiddelech," the piece he wanted to play for the talent show.

"Abe Schwartz's Orchestra couldn't have done it better!" Uncle Maxwell said after Benny finished. "Speaking of bands, how goes the search?"

"It's stalled. I've got a drummer and a clarinetist, but finding an accordion player is tough."

"I know you said to butt out, but I do know somebody who might be able to help."

After his conversation with Jennifer, Benny did want to start practicing. But he felt using a ringer—a professional—would look odd. And he could hear what Jason would say: "You amateurs needed a widdle help, huh? Couldn't do it yourself?"

"I really need to find someone closer to my age," Benny said.

"Tell you what. Let's go meet my buddy and see if he's available. If so, you might be able to see how your group cooks together. Sometimes even the best musicians don't quite gel right from the start."

Uncle Maxwell pointed to a photograph of an accordion player. "That's Al. Our paths haven't crossed for a few years, but I heard he owns a shop in town. It's right in your neighborhood."

"I guess meeting him can't hurt."

≳ ♪ ≲

"Why are we stopping here?" Benny asked as his uncle parked the car in front of Alistair's Oddities.

"This is where Al lives," Uncle Maxwell said.

"I come into Alistair's shop all the time. He's *my* friend, too."

"Well, well, what a small world!" Uncle Maxwell said as they walked inside.

"BENNNY!" Alistair shouted. "And MAXXXIE? How ya been?" He gave his old friend a bear hug.

"You know, fiddlin' here, fiddlin' there," Uncle Maxwell said. "I see you already know my nephew."

"Benny is one of my best customers. A pinball wizard, too. And he sure loves his klezmer."

"I've taught him everything I know. You should hear him play the violin. He's got serious chops."

Alistair looked over at the crates of albums where Benny was inspecting the latest arrivals.

"Benny, you've been holding out on me," he said, slightly hurt.

"It's been kind of a secret—up until now."

"Kind of?"

"Okay, a total secret."

For a few minutes Uncle Maxwell and Alistair traded stories. They talked about gigs where the pay was good, the music hot, the food plentiful, and people danced to exhaustion. Then there were the performances where the band was ignored, and when they left with less money in their pockets than when they had arrived.

Alistair had played the accordion in a Scottish band called Tartan Sauce. Whenever the regular fiddler couldn't make it, he would call Maxwell to play the band's set of Scottish jigs and hornpipes.

"You wouldn't believe how difficult it was finding a kilt large enough to fit him," Alistair said. "And he insisted on wearing that brown fedora!"

When Maxwell's klezmer ensemble needed a replacement accordion player, they could always count on Alistair.

"Remember that Rosenstein bar mitzvah you asked me to sit in on?" Alistair said.

"How could I forget it? During the dance, the bar mitzvah boy fell off the chair…."

"… and right onto the sheet cake!"

The two laughed as Benny waited.

"So what brings you here, Benny? Looking for more records?" Alistair asked.

Benny explained that he needed an accordion player as a stand-in to help his klezmer band start practicing. Alistair's expression turned somber. He lifted his right hand to reveal three gnarled fingers.

"My accordion-playing days are over. A refrigerator fell off a gurney when I was moving it to the back room a few years ago. This here is my bionic baby, held together with pins and screws. It's functional but not nimble enough to fly over any keyboard."

"Sorry, Al, I had no idea," Uncle Maxwell said.

"No apologies necessary. It is what it is. I still have music in my life. My record player. My albums. My memories. And I'm teaching my nephew Stuart a few tricks of the trade, though he hardly needs it. He and Sis live above the shop. For a sixth-grader, he can really play."

"Play what?" Benny asked.

"The accordion."

Benny's eyes widened as he looked at his uncle in disbelief.

"You have a nephew who plays the accordion and lives upstairs?" Benny said.

"Yeah, his parents divorced and Sis moved up here from Louisiana. They're staying with me for a few months until they can get on their feet. He goes to a private school in the burbs."

"Can I meet him?"

"Sure, but I don't think Stuart will be a good fit for your band." Alistair pressed a buzzer beneath the counter.

"Why not?"

"You'll see."

♫

"So what's in it for me?" Stuart asked. He leaned against the pinball machine as Benny pulled back the plunger.

Stuart LeBlanc was short and stocky. A stiff black Mohawk ran down the center of his head. His impressive arm muscles seemed to say, "Yes, I can hold an accordion, and don't mess with me if you know what's good for you." A wad of bubble gum packed one cheek, making him look like a lopsided chipmunk with an attitude.

Benny knew there was little he could offer Stuart. No money. No promise of glory. Only the high probability of being made fun of if the band flopped at the talent show.

"See, I'm already in several bands," Stuart said, pink gum juice dripping from the side of his mouth. "A polka band. A rock band. A Zydeco group. I'm in demand. And get paid *real* money. I don't have time for a little kiddie talent show." He grinned, revealing a slight chip in one of his front teeth.

The words "little kiddie" made Benny bristle, especially

since he stood two heads taller than Stuart. After listening to him brag about past gigs, Benny wasn't sure if recruiting him was worth the effort. But to complete his band, he kept trying.

"Our klezmer band has great musicians, too. I'm the fiddler. Royce plays the clarinet...."

"I played some klezmer a long time ago—back in first grade—or was it in preschool? Lots of minor chords. Very repetitive. Background music mainly. By the way, nice hat."

Stuart watched Benny's ball go down a side lane and looked up at the score. "Nice try. I doubled that score the first time I played this machine, isn't that right, Uncle Alistair?"

Benny fumed. He balled up his right hand, his fingers coiling together to form a fist. These were the same fingers that lovingly caressed his violin. The same fingers that yearned to hold Jennifer's hand. Out of respect for Alistair, he stood in place and remained silent.

"Well, gotta go," Stuart said. "Big gig tomorrow night." He turned and stomped up the stairs—an F-5 tornado touching down before disappearing into the sky. Within minutes, the sound of an accordion playing a Cajun-tinged version of "Jambalaya" drifted down from the apartment above. Stuart *was* an exceptional musician, which made Benny even angrier.

"Is he always like that?" Benny asked.

"Didn't used to be, before the divorce," Alistair said.

"It's a shame. He's got all the mechanics of the accordion down, but right now he's missing the joy."

"Tough luck, Benny," Uncle Maxwell said.

"Well, you're welcome to use my shop to practice. The acoustics are great here, and there's an old kit your drummer can use. I may not be able to play, but I'd be happy to give you guys some pointers."

"Thanks for the offer. I'll let the band know."

$\xi \, \flat \, \xi$

On the ride home, Uncle Maxwell could tell Benny was steaming.

"There's a Yiddish word for people like Stuart— *oysshteler*," Uncle Maxwell said.

"Is it similar to *schmendrick?*" Benny heard his parents shout this word at the television during the evening news.

"Close but not quite. An *oysshteler* is a know-it-all. A show-off."

"He's a *schmendrick,* too. A fool. And he knows nothing about klezmer."

"Maybe you'll have to teach him."

$\xi \, \flat \, \xi$

Later, in his bedroom, Benny recalled Uncle Maxwell telling one of Moshe's stories about a rival fiddler named Yossef.

In my day I played with a lot of braggarts, but Yossef topped them all. If I had two rubles in my pocket, he had three. If I had three, he had four. At least that's what he'd say.

If I played at a wedding attended by one hundred people, he played a party with three hundred, no, four hundred—all of whom said they'd never heard such a majestic sound, as if Gideon himself had traded in his trumpet for a fiddle.

I had to admit, Yossef played magnificently. But, oy, was he insufferable!

One sunny morning Yossef boasted that he had played three days and three nights straight without taking a single break. Never put his fiddle down once. That was the final straw. Improbable, I said. No, impossible. So I challenged him right then and there to a contest to see who could play the longest.

We began playing freylekhs and bulgars, doinas and shers—pulling out every tune we knew. With both of us sawing away at different pieces at the same time, the music sounded bitter. Screechy. Unlistenable.

By noon the hot sun burned our necks and baked our fiddles. Neither of us would quit.

Later the sky opened up and it began to rain. Water dripped off our hats, down our necks, and straight into the f-holes of our fiddles.

By now the music sounded bland, like herring without onions. Yet we refused to stop.

Finally, as the first star appeared in the darkening sky, Yossef paused and put down his instrument.

"You win, Moshe. I cannot play another note."

For a moment I felt a swell of pride until I looked into my opponent's eyes. What riches had I gained from my victory? Only a soggy bow, waterlogged boots, burned skin, throbbing legs, and a sore arm. I was turning to leave when Yossef tugged on my damp shirt.

"How about we try one more tune, together this time?"

And we did, a sweet melody that filled both our souls.

Benny had never understood the point of this story, other than the obvious: Don't play your fiddle in the rain!

Should I challenge Stuart to a duel? His accordion versus my fiddle? Is that the point? Then he remembered how his uncle ended the story.

"Don't give up on a good musician just because they're a pain in the *tuches*. Nobody fiddles that well without having experienced a little sorrow in their lives."

One more chance, Stuart. I'll give you one more chance, Benny said to himself, flicking off the lights. As he closed his eyes, he smiled at the vision of his uncle wearing a kilt in public.

♪

Benny texted Jennifer and Royce.

Benny: Snagged a place to practice. Also have a lead on an accordion player.

Jennifer: YES!!!!

Royce: Time to see what we've got!

Benny: Just emailed you an MP3 and sheet music for "Tantz, Tantz Yiddelech!"

Jennifer: Watch out, Jason, here we come!

♫ **12** ♫

Benny envisioned "Tantz, Tantz Yiddelech" beginning with the fiddle playing a slow, improvised solo, only hinting at the tune's catchy melody. The second time through, the clarinet would harmonize with the fiddle, pushing the tempo just a bit. Then the drums would creep in—first light taps on the snare shifting to cymbal crashes and thunderous beats on the toms, the deeper-sounding drums. Unleashed, the band would rev up to maximum speed by the fifth time through.

"We'll hold the final note as long as possible—drums bashing, clarinet trilling, and fiddle playing up and down the fingerboard," Benny said, wildly moving his arms to demonstrate how he heard the song's chaotic conclusion. "I'll lift my fiddle slightly. That will mean it's time for the final short note, a stinger. It'll be like a giant exclamation mark."

"I get it, B-Man," Royce said. "But it'd be cool to start the song extra fast. You know, blow 'em away from the start. The title of the tune means 'Dance, Dance Jews.' Let's get the audience up and moving right away."

Benny stood firm. "No, the melody should sink in first. Trust me. I've thought a lot about this."

"How about starting with a slow but loud one-two-three-four beat on the drums to get the crowd clapping," Jennifer said, spinning her drumsticks.

"I can hear it," Royce said. "But still not fast enough for me."

An hour elapsed and Benny Feldman's All-Star Klezmer Band had yet to play its first measure together.

"Let's try it my way first. Just for now," Benny said.

He began playing alone, pulling heart-wrenching tones out of his fiddle. Royce and Jennifer jumped in as Benny had suggested. The music plodded along, slowed down, sped up, jerked, stopped, and lurched forward again. Their awkward journey ended with a cymbal crash and an ear-splitting clarinet squeak, followed by an uncomfortable moment of silence. The trio looked at each other, unsure of what to say.

To Benny, their playing sounded like an auto accident—three musicians using different Google directions to arrive at the same intersection, ramming headfirst as airbags exploded and windshields shattered.

Jennifer remembered her mother's words on the first day of kindergarten: "If you don't have anything nice to say, don't say anything at all." So she kept quiet.

Royce readjusted the joints and mouthpiece of his

clarinet and practiced a *krecht*, a klezmer moaning sound. Jennifer tightened the snare drum head. Benny retuned his fiddle and applied a thin layer of rosin to his bow.

Then they tried it again, using Royce's idea for the tune. The results were the same.

The three soon realized the arrangement wasn't the problem. They were.

Alistair intervened. "You're all playing the notes, but you're not using the most important instrument of all— your ears."

Royce placed his clarinet's bell against the side of his head. "Like this?"

"Can you see why he got kicked out of band class?" Jennifer said.

"Imagine you're having a three-way conversation," Alistair continued. "Lay back when someone else is speaking. Don't interrupt unless you have something valuable to say. Roar when the spotlight hits you. And don't be afraid to express your own opinion."

"I'm not following you," Benny said.

"Listen to each other!"

"Got it."

They muddled through the tune a third time, then a fourth and a fifth. They were listening, but everyone was still speaking a different language.

But on the sixth try, Benny felt it. The band clicked, just a little, like a switch turning on a reading lamp. Benny Feldman's All-Star Klezmer Band had taken a small step forward, mostly staying in tempo and occasionally blending together in the way Benny had imagined. What began as an unpolished rock had turned, in Alistair's words, "into an unpolished rock with potential."

And there's still time to make us shine like a diamond, Benny thought.

In between playing, Benny tossed his fedora onto Jennifer's head. Royce made the others howl by tootling the old *Batman* theme on his clarinet using klezmer clucking noises. Jennifer balanced a drumstick on her nose and told jokes she had learned from her father.

"What do you get when you drop a piano in a mine shaft?"

Royce knew that one: "A flat miner."

"I've got another," Jennifer said. "Why did the clarinetist end up in the storage room?"

No answers.

"Because he was in T-R-E-B-L-E."

"That is B-A-D, J-Kom," Royce laughed.

"Finally, words I recognize," Benny said.

Lost in the moment, they all failed to notice Stuart standing off to the side. His head barely poked above the black-and-white accordion strapped to his chest. It looked as if the instrument had eaten him alive.

"I heard you from upstairs. Sounds like you could use my help." He pulled up a chair and settled in next to Royce.

"Who is this guy?" Jennifer whispered to Benny.

"I'll explain later," he said.

Benny handed Stuart the sheet music, but he waved it away. "Don't need it. Learned it by listening through the furnace vent. Key of A minor, like that flat guy in the mine shaft. Nothing too complicated. Come on, time's wasting."

Here goes, Benny thought, expecting a four-way collision.

A mournful, rich vibrato sounding like a woman weeping rose from Benny's fiddle. Royce joined in perfect harmony. Stuart listened and waited before adding his voice to the discussion. He handled the accordion as if it was a living, breathing extension of his body, squeezing out perfect chords that made Benny's heart soar. His right hand raced up and down the keyboard while his left worked the buttons. Driven by the pulsating sound of the accordion's bass notes, Jennifer attacked the drums. The band responded by playing with a wild abandon that rattled the store's shelves.

After the final note faded, the four held their breath, as if exhaling would end the magic. Benny wanted the moment to last forever.

Stuart stood up and stretched. "That's how it's done, folks."

Now more than ever, Benny wanted Stuart in the band. He *had* to have Stuart in the band. "Will you join us, Stuart? I know you're busy…."

"Way to go, Stu-ccordion!" Jennifer said.

"Man, didn't you feel it? We've got something P-R-O-D-I-G-I-O-U-S here!" Royce said.

"What's with the spelling?" Stuart asked.

"Can't help it. I'm in training for the spelling bee."

Stuart yawned. "I'll think about joining the band, but probably N-O-T."

≥ ♪ ≤

Benny could not get the gum-chewing accordion player out of his mind. He texted the band:

I'm asking Stuart to go with us to the convention.

Royce: r u crazy?

Jennifer: A bribe so he'll join the band?

Benny: No, I think he needs us.

Jennifer: He needs US?

Royce: Seems like he's doing fine on his own.

Jennifer: He'll probably say no.

Royce: Highly likely.

♪**13**♪

Benny, Ollie, Jennifer, and Royce met Stuart in front of the Samuel P. Ardmore Convention Center.

"Glad you could make it," Benny said.

"Not much else to do in this town on a Saturday afternoon. Good way to kill a few hours. The last convention I went to in New Orleans was five times as big as this," Stuart said.

"Whatever," Jennifer sighed.

Ollie assumed that the convention would be a good chance to catch up with Benny. They hadn't spent time together in weeks. Before Ollie could mention the Monster-Thon and the new frisbee he had bought, Benny swung around and faced his bandmates.

"I've got some new ideas for 'Tantz, Tantz Yiddelech,'" he said.

By the time Benny turned back around ten minutes later, Ollie had forgotten what he wanted to say. He shuffled to the entrance in silence.

Inside, costumed characters from Royce's favorite comic books milled about: the Hulk, the Thing, the Mighty Thor, Spiderman, Wolverine, and scores more.

"This is awesome!" Royce said as he posed for pictures with Wonder Woman.

"I wonder if the rootin' tootin' Chipster is here," Jennifer said.

"You mean the Defender of Truth, Justice, and All That Is Salty?" Benny replied.

Weaving through the maze of vendors, Benny and his guests made their way to the arcade. Using the rolls of quarters Benny gave them, they split up to play their favorite games.

In the center of the room stood a pair of the most advanced pinball machines Benny had ever seen—the Blast-Off 2079. Each table had six flippers, two upper levels, a third underground level, twisting habitrails, narrow ramps, multiple ball modes, a spaceship that cracked open to reveal a three-headed alien, and a computerized voice that mocked the player's mistakes.

Alistair's winking genie machine is "Twinkle, Twinkle Little Star." The Blast-Off 2079 is a Mahler symphony, Benny thought.

A sign-up sheet hung next to one of the machines. It read: "One-Ball Tournament—3:00 p.m." *JASON THE ADJUDICATOR* was scrawled in slanted letters on the top line.

There was no doubt in Benny's mind. *That's Jason Conroy. He's here. Somewhere in the building. But where?*

Benny felt a tap on his shoulder. He turned around and stood before the Adjudicator himself, along with the rest of the Neanderthal Four.

"Shouldn't you be home practicing with your band?" Jason said. He wore a Neanderthal Four T-shirt showing the band's name chiseled in stone.

Benny wasn't surprised that Jason was there. Practically all of Sieberling School attended the convention. But his sudden appearance shook Benny. After the potato chip factory tour, Benny had changed his survival tip of "Blend into the background" to "Stand your ground." This, however, was too close for comfort. He backed up three steps before speaking.

"My band is here," Benny said, puffing out his chest.

"Sure it is. You and that drummer."

Benny began to boil. He took three steps forward, making Jason retreat.

"She's not 'that drummer.' She's J-Kom, you caveman!" he muttered under his breath.

Looking up from a Centipede console, Jennifer spied Jason and his crew surrounding Benny. She gathered up Royce, Ollie, and Stuart and hurried to Benny's side. Standing a few feet apart, the two bands silently assessed each other. The Neanderthal Four glared at Benny and his group, amazed they would dare to compete with them.

Benny recognized Jason's band: Theresa Charleton, keyboard player and winner of the district piano competition; "Sticks" McCracken, an eighth-grade drummer who wore a Keith Moon T-shirt and a perpetual scowl; and Filbert Jones, whose thumping bass lines from last year's talent show still haunted Benny's dreams.

Jason evaluated Benny's band. The look on his face seemed to say, "I see no major threat. The first-place trophy is ours for the taking."

"So *this* is the Amazing Exploding Grape Band?" Jason said.

"Exploding grape?" Stuart said. "What's he talking about? Who are these guys?"

"Cool it, Stuart," Benny said.

"Stoo-art?" Jason drawled. "You've recruited Stuart Little to be in your band? Hey, Stuart Little, want a piece of cheese?" Every third-grader at Sieberling School was required to read *Stuart Little,* the story of the plucky mouse. It had been one of Benny's favorites—until now.

Stuart's face flushed. He let out a low growl, dropped his head, and charged. Ollie and Jennifer grabbed his shirttails and held on. Benny and Royce jumped in front to block his path. They knew if Stuart tackled Jason like a blitzing linebacker, it would get them all kicked out of the convention.

"Why are you being so B-E-L-L-I-G-E-R-E-N-T?" Royce asked, pointing at Jason.

Jason turned to Sticks for a translation. "I don't know what it means, but it sounds like he just dissed you. I'd give him a K-A-P-O-W right in the kisser."

"Not worth my time. See you losers later," Jason said, leading his band out of the arcade room.

Royce and Stuart stood shocked, the sound of buzzers and blips flooding their ears.

"So now you've met Jason," Benny sighed.

"Remember when I said I didn't want to destroy anyone?" Royce asked.

"Yes," Benny said.

"I take it back. I want to A-N-N-I-H-I-L-A-T-E Jason and the Neanderthal Four!"

"If that means what I think it means, then I'm in," Stuart said. "I want to A-N-N-I- ... oh ... whatever ... every last one of them!"

♩ ♪ ♩

Sharing a cheese pizza in the food court, Benny filled in Royce and Stuart about his history with Jason. The Sabbath play. The nickname. The stage fright. The basketball game. It all came flooding out. He found the more he told the exploding grape saga to others, the easier it became.

"I didn't mean to ruin everyone's day," Benny said. "But you all have a right to know. If you decide to bail on the band and the talent show, I'll understand."

Stuart remained silent, still stinging from Jason's comments.

"I'm with you, Benny!" Royce said.

"Me too!" Jennifer added.

Jennifer, Royce, and Benny raised their glasses filled with root beer and clinked them together. In spite of the scene in the arcade, Benny was excited by the thought that, against all odds, the pieces of his klezmer band were falling into place. Ollie sat quietly with his arms crossed. He had barely uttered a word all day.

Stuart bowed his head and softly said, "I lied."

"About joining the band?" Benny asked.

"No, about playing in other bands. About being in demand. I lied to impress you."

"Why? You're good enough to play with anybody," Jennifer said.

"I thought you would be like the rest of them."

"Who's *them*?" Royce asked.

"The ones who call me Stuart Little. Mouse Boy. Cheese Eater. I've never told anyone at school I play the accordion. That would just give them another reason to make fun of me."

"We'd never do that, right guys?" Jennifer said, wiping her eyes. The boys nodded.

"When I came down with the accordion at my uncle's shop, it wasn't because I heard the music. It was because I heard you having fun. Joking around. I wanted to be part of it. I wasn't sure then, but I am now. I *want* to be in the band."

"Hey, Stuart, what do you call a cow that plays the accordion?" Jennifer asked.

"Huh?"

"What do you call a cow that plays the accordion?"

"No idea."

"A moo-sician."

Stuart groaned as Royce raised his glass. "Now it's official. Once J-Kom puts you in one of her jokes, there's no turning back. Let's try this toast again. To the band!"

"To the band!" they said as one.

None of them noticed Ollie quietly slipping off into the crowd.

"Let's go back to the arcade room," Benny said. "There's something I need to do."

≥ ♪ ≤

Benny reached into his pocket and pulled out the black felt-tip marker he had used weeks ago to write "Benny Feldman's All-Star Klezmer Band." This time he wrote "B-MAN" on the bottom line of the One-Ball Tournament registration sheet. He adjusted his fedora and straightened his shoulders.

"*Nobody* calls us losers," he said.

Tournament organizers split the contestants into two brackets displayed on a video screen above the Blast-Off 2079s. Winners of each round would advance to the next opponent until only two competitors remained to battle for the championship. The first-place winner would receive a trophy and a pass to next year's convention. The second-place finisher would go home with a coupon book to Frankie's House of Corndogs, one of the convention sponsors.

"I'd enter, but it wouldn't be fair. I totally rule this machine," Stuart bragged.

"Are you for real?" Royce sighed.

"Gotcha! Just kidding! I'm really lousy at pinball."

"Maybe we should have let Jason and his band pummel you," Jennifer said.

Benny analyzed the Blast-Off 2079. Playing it would be like sight-reading a piece of music he had never heard.

If I can win the first couple of rounds, I might have a chance. Give me fifteen minutes and I'll be playing this table like I'm headlining at Carnegie Hall.

A woman dressed as Princess Leia stepped to the microphone: "Ladies, gentlemen, wizards, and inhabitants of galaxies light years away, I present to you our epic, astro-stupendooouuus One-Ball Tournament—sponsored by Frankie's House of Corndogs at the corner of Fifth and Main, next to Speedy Wash!"

The crowd cheered. Benny flexed his long fingers like a Jedi itching to reach for his light saber and take on a legion of stormtroopers. Jason, yawning and looking bored, stood with his band on the other side of the semicircle around the machines.

"And now, our first competitors on their trek to one-ball glory—B-Man and Twirl-Girl!"

Benny glanced to his left. It was Amanda Grayson.

The two walked up to the machines. "This must be my lucky day," Amanda said, glaring at Benny.

A red light flashed. They simultaneously pulled back the plungers and launched their balls. "PREPARE TO MEET YOUR DOOM, MU-HA-HA," a deep voice boomed from each table. The sound surprised Benny. He hit the top right flipper in time to send the ball up a lit ramp where it pinged between bumpers. A spinning galaxy caught the ball and flung it dead center to the bottom. "FEEL MY PITILESS WRATH!" the voice roared.

I lost! In the first round! And to Twirl-Girl Grayson! I'm swearing off sign-up sheets!

"And our first-round winner is ... B-Man!" Princess Leia announced.

It turned out to be Benny's lucky day. A muscular ninth-grader dressed as Aquaman had caught Amanda's eye, causing her to lose focus and fail to score a single point.

"You'll be sorry," Amanda hissed at Benny before she stomped away.

Jennifer, Stuart, and Royce gave Benny high-fives. Ollie was nowhere to be seen.

"I've got to ramp up my game to stay in this," Benny said. "This machine is fast!"

"Feel the Force, young B-Man," Stuart said, winking at Princess Leia.

Benny struggled at first, narrowly winning the next few

matchups as he learned the nuances of the machine. But by the fourth round, he was no longer sight-reading. He had memorized the table. A growing crowd of onlookers marveled at his dexterity as he doubled and then tripled his opponents' scores.

Jason dispatched each challenger with ease as young and old competitors alike suffered defeat against his pinball prowess. After each victory he calmly gave a thumbs-up to his band. One after the other, contestants slinked away after being beaten.

A piercing buzzer blared. Princess Leia parted the crowd and grabbed the microphone: "Ladies, gentlemen, super-villains, and denizens of Neptopia, I present to you our two intergalactic survivors—B-Man and Jason the Adjudicator!"

Jason raised both arms, soaking up the cheers. Benny hadn't noticed until now that the crowd around the machines had swelled to eight rows deep. He trembled as the pizza and root beer from lunch gurgled in his stomach.

I'm going to pass out right here on the floor of the Samuel P. Ardmore Convention Center ... in ... front ... of... EVERYBODY!

A cool hand slipped into Benny's palm, slender fingers intertwining with his. "You *can* do this, B-Man," Jennifer whispered into his ear. "You *can* do this."

Jason and Benny strode to their machines, two asteroids hurtling toward each other at light speed.

♪

The red light flashed. Benny and Jason pulled back the plungers and released, sending their balls rocketing into the machines' upper realms.

Jason grabbed a fast lead, repeatedly flicking his ball up a bonus ramp. The orange digital tally on his machine reached one million, then two, then three. Benny stayed under the 100,000 mark, failing to hit the sweet spots that would send his score soaring into the stratosphere.

Chants of "JASON! JASON! JASON!" echoed on Benny's left. "B-MAN! B-MAN! B-MAN!" rumbled on his right.

A blinking message appeared on Benny's machine: "Hit the Black Hole for Bonus, Good for Five Seconds."

Benny eyed his target, a small round depression at the top of the machine hidden behind a ramp and three bumpers. No straight shot. Catching the ball on a left flipper, he banked it off a side slingshot, finessing it through a narrow passageway. With a satisfying plink, it rolled squarely into the black hole.

The machine went pitch black. One … two … three seconds ticked by. Suddenly, the deep voice bellowed an agonizing "NOOOOOOO!"

The Blast-Off 2079 lit up, flashing in red, green, purple, and yellow. The black hole spewed five bonus balls onto the playing field. Benny's hands furiously kept each one careening from side to side. His score skyrocketed: five million … ten … fifteen … thirty.

Benny caught a glimpse of Jason. His opponent. His tormenter. Jason was sweating. Benny saw panic in his eyes. Jason was cornered, trapped, rocking on his back.

The Amazing Exploding Grape will be put to rest, Benny thought. *The nightmare over. It will end here. End now.*

Benny looked up to see his final score. It was the most he had ever tallied on a single ball:

B-MAN
46,876,681

He imagined the news being posted online: "Klezmer Kid Conquers Conroy!" Over the loudspeaker came Princess Leia's voice: "AND THE WINNER OF THE ONE-BALL TOURNAMENT—JASON THE ADJUDICATOR!"

Benny shot another glance at the video screen and stared in disbelief:

JASON THE ADJUDICATOR
46,876,783

I lost by 102 points! Only 102 points!

Jason held the trophy aloft as Benny received the coupon book. Head down, he walked back to his band.

"Way to make him sweat," Stuart shouted loud enough for Jason to hear.

"Great game!" Royce said, slapping Benny on the back.

"I knew you could do it," Jennifer said.

"But I lost."

"I'm not talking about winning. I'm talking about showing everyone who you are."

This time, Benny took Jennifer's hand and squeezed it tight.

"Who's up for some free corndogs?" Benny asked.

♪14♪

In his room, klezmer tunes stayed offline in Benny's brain. Closing his eyes, all he saw was Jennifer. J-Kom. The girl with the red horn-rimmed glasses. The one who had given him a cool nickname. Who loved jazz. Played the drums. Stood up to Jason.

WHO HELD MY HAND!!!

She was the first. His mother and aunts didn't count. Neither did Karen the Kiddush Cup or Amanda Grayson, who was forced to be his square dance partner in second-grade gym class. After the promenade she ran to the girls' restroom screaming about washing away the "grape cooties."

Benny recalled one of Uncle Maxwell's stories. He stared hard at the black-and-white photo of Moshe and imagined his great-great-grandfather's cold expression melting into a warm smile.

I met young ladies traveling from town to town. None paid much attention to me. I was a scrawny and shy musician with nothing to offer but my music. I let my fiddle speak for me.

Then one day, playing a wedding in Sebastopol, I noticed a young lady locking eyes with me every time she danced past the band. She was smiling—at me! I asked myself, was this my imagination? She must be looking at Yankel the cellist. That I could understand. Or Shlomo the drummer. But Moshe, the poor fiddler from Minsk? It couldn't be.

During a break, she walked up to the band, brushing past Yankel and Shlomo. "You play the violin beautifully," she said. "My name is Minna Weiss."

Tongue-tied, I could hardly muster the courage to say my name.

"Your hands!" Minna cupped my blistered and bleeding palms in hers. I had ugly hands. Rough and calloused hands that no one could cherish. A klezmer fiddler's hands. She looked down at them in bewilderment, wondering how hands so scarred could produce music so exquisite.

Minna dipped her lace handkerchief in a pitcher of water and gently dabbed away the blood.

That was the first time I held your great-great-grandmother's hand, or rather, she held mine. In that moment, my life began.

Benny's phone sounded.

I don't want to hang with you anymore, Ollie texted.

Benny felt queasy. Why???

You don't need me. You have a klezmer band. A girlfriend. New buds. Don't text back.

Benny turned to Moshe. "Why isn't anything easy?"

Get used to it. Yankel never talked to me again either.

≥ ♫ ≤

Sitting at the kitchen table, Benny jabbed at his scrambled eggs and French toast.

"Is there something you need to tell me?" Mrs. Feldman asked.

"Benny came in second at the pinball tournament!" Sam interjected. "There's a picture of him online. It says, 'Benny Goes Bust!' How cool is that? He's famous!"

"One more word, Sam, and you'll be in your room until your ride to Sunday school comes."

"What did I say? Did you also know Benny has a *girlfriend*?"

"That's it! Go!"

Sam dragged his feet up the stairs, grumbling with each step.

As an attorney, Mrs. Feldman cross-examined witnesses all the time. She had a sixth sense for telling when someone was withholding critical information. Benny knew it was useless to resist.

"Ollie doesn't want to be my friend anymore. I kind of ignored him at the convention yesterday," Benny said.

"Kind of?"

"Well ... completely. He left without even saying goodbye."

"Can't you talk to him? Sort out this misunderstanding?"

"Ollie told me not to contact him. He thinks because I'm part of a band and have a girlfriend that I don't need him anymore."

"A girlfriend? So Sam wasn't making up stories?"

"No, Mom. Jennifer and I held hands. I guess that means she's my girlfriend."

"I'd say the evidence is strong."

"Why do bad things always seem to follow good things?"

"In science you'll learn Newton's Third Law of Physics: 'Every action has an equal and opposite reaction.' In Jewish terms it means you should savor the happy times because trouble may be lurking around the corner."

"That doesn't help, Mom," Benny said.

"Don't worry, Ollie will come back. Give him time. Everything should return to normal once the talent show is over."

"I hope you're right."

♪ **15** ♪

Benny pinned down his blue-and-white yarmulke and did his best to tune out the classmates sitting behind him in Beth El's chapel. They were discussing the Cleveland Browns upcoming game against the Pittsburgh Steelers and gossiping about the latest news unfolding in the world of pre-teen romance. He thought he heard his name whispered once or twice but chose not to glance back.

It looked like the start of another typical day at synagogue. Then Cantor Berkowitz addressed the school.

"Listen up, sixth-graders! Mrs. Rosenstein's car won't start. That means you'll be stuck with me. I don't have a lesson plan, so we'll just have to wing it."

So much for typical, Benny thought.

Benny liked Cantor Berkowitz. He was a short, bearded man in his late twenties who had been hired about a year ago. The cantor's mellow baritone made emerging from a warm bed on a cold January morning a little less difficult.

Benny loved singing along to the cantor's heartfelt version of "Adon Olom" and rousing rendition of "Ein Keloheinu," which signaled the end of the service.

What Benny didn't like was the idea of "winging" anything. Mrs. Rosenstein would have drilled the class on Hebrew vocabulary. And that would have been fine. But Cantor Berkowitz was a wildcard. Sam had told Benny that last Sunday he had turned his fourth-grade class into *American Idol,* making the students stand up and sing their favorite songs.

In Benny's mind, "winging it" could mean, "Time for karaoke!" or "Let's arm wrestle. You and Jason go first."

Benny looked around the chapel, which was much smaller than the main sanctuary. A handful of congregants prayed among the students who filled five wooden pews facing the bima. Winter sunlight streamed through the stained-glass windows along the eastern wall, bathing the space in colored light.

Benny stared at the embroidered cover on the ark doors. It depicted a scene from the story of Noah and the Flood. A rainbow arched above lions, toucans, alligators, bison, and other paired animals stepping onto dry land. He homed in on the two giraffes towering above the others.

A toucan can hide in a mango tree. A chameleon can camouflage itself against any surface. An alligator can disappear under water. But a giraffe? How does a giraffe blend in?

When the service ended, the rest of the students and teachers filed to their classrooms. The sixth-graders remained in their seats.

Cantor Berkowitz pulled out his acoustic guitar. "Ready for some fun?" he asked.

Benny groaned and offered a silent prayer: *Oh, Lord, please get me through the next hour without having to get up in front of the class. If so, I promise to eat my zucchinis and mushrooms next time without complaining.* He shifted to a seat near the door in case he had to make an emergency exit. *A giraffe can't hide, but it sure as heck can run from danger.*

"Now it's time to play Jewish Music Jeopardy!" Cantor Berkowitz said, strumming a G chord.

This doesn't sound good. Benny eyed the open door as if a lion were about to lunge at him from behind the lectern.

"Here's how it works. I'll start playing a tune on my guitar. As soon as you know it, raise your hand and shout out the name of the song or the artist who either wrote or performed it. Here's a hint: They're all Jewish."

Benny grinned. *This* he could handle. This *did* sound like fun.

"What do we win?" Jason asked, crossing his arms.

"Good question. You will win the satisfaction of realizing how the Jewish people have made vast contributions to music and knowing that your lives are richer because of it."

Jason snorted. "What? No trophy? No prize money?"

"Who do I look like? Alex Trebek? Let's begin. I'll start

with an easy one." He picked a D, D, F#, E♭, and D on his guitar and began to sing, "Ha-va—"

Before the cantor got the next word out, every hand in the class shot up. "Hava Nagila!" they all shouted.

"Well done, contestants!"

Cantor Berkowitz strummed another song. Jason raised his hand. "God Bless America," he said.

"And who wrote it?"

"Irving Berlin," Benny blurted out. "He was born in 1888. His father was a cantor in Russia before coming to the United States!"

"Bravo! Bonus points for Benny!"

From that moment on Benny dominated the game, rattling off titles and performers in quick-fire succession: "You've Got a Friend"—Carole King; "Bridge Over Troubled Water"—Simon and Garfunkel; "Just Give Me a Reason"—Pink; "Blowing in the Wind"—Bob Dylan; "Hallelujah"—Leonard Cohen; "Over the Rainbow"— Harold Arlen and Yip Harburg; "The Wedding March"— Felix Mendelssohn; "Evergreen"—Barbra Streisand; "Maria"—Leonard Bernstein and Stephen Sondheim. No matter what the cantor played, old or new, Benny knew the answer and a fact about the musician.

Jason interjected wild guesses to throw Benny off his unstoppable run. Karen Neumar sneered at Benny as if he belonged in a carnival sideshow. The Grossman twins nodded off to sleep.

"We have time for one more," Cantor Berkowitz said,

glancing at the clock. He gave Benny a look as if to say, "You couldn't possibly know this one."

After only five notes, Benny calmly answered, "Tantz, Tantz Yiddelech."

≳ ♪ ≲

As the class left to catch their rides, Cantor Berkowitz waved Benny over. "Your performance in class was extraordinary," he said. "How did you know all that music?"

"I listen to a lot of music. My Uncle Maxwell makes sure I hear all different kinds. And when a song is by a Jewish musician, he always points it out so I'll be proud of who I am."

"But how did you know 'Tantz, Tantz Yiddelech'? I would have bet a million dollars that one would have stumped you."

"It's a long story."

"Give me the short version."

"I'm a fiddler in a klezmer band. Up to now we've only practiced. In March we're going to play 'Tantz, Tantz Yiddelech' at my school talent show."

"I'll mark it on my calendar."

"That's alright. You don't have to come."

"Why not?"

Because I'm still terrified of performing, and I don't want you to see me make a fool of myself.

"It's just a school talent show. No big deal," Benny said.

"Well, I'll try to make it anyway." Cantor Berkowitz looked hard at the boy with the blue-and-white yarmulke. He had helped enough petrified bar and bat mitzvah students to recognize the troubled expression shadowing Benny's face. "Is there something I can help you with?"

"No," Benny said. He got up to leave but turned before he reached the chapel door. "Do you have any advice about performing? I'm a little nervous about getting on stage."

"I used to have stage fright, too. In cantorial school I learned my job wasn't to be the star of the show, but to be a glimmer in a bigger constellation. Once during Kol Nidre services I could barely make a peep because of a bad case of laryngitis. It didn't matter. That night every congregant sang and carried me along. How could I be frightened when so many people were there to catch me if I fell?"

"I think I understand. Thank you," Benny said.

"Come on, let's do one last song," Cantor Berkowitz said, strumming his guitar. "Know this one, Benny?"

"Yes," he said. "'I'm a Believer' by Neil Diamond."

As he got in the car to go home, Benny realized what had just happened:

I finally beat Jason at something. I finally won. Next stop, the talent show!

♪

Before practice began in the back of Alistair's Oddities, Benny made an announcement: "Benny Feldman's All-Star Klezmer Band will not be performing at the Sieberling School talent show."

Jennifer halted a snare roll. Royce stopped cleaning his mouthpiece. Stuart peeked out over his accordion as a discordant wheeze drained from its bellows.

"You're kidding, right?" Royce asked.

"We've come too far to quit now," Stuart said.

"I'm not kidding and I'm not talking about quitting," Benny said. "I want *us* to play but with another name."

"B-Man, what are you driving at?" Jennifer asked, punctuating her words with a cymbal splash.

"I'm saying our band name should be about *all* of us, not just me. Any ideas?"

"The Klez Dispensers!" Stuart said. "Like the candy dispensers but with music."

"Great name, but it's been taken," Benny said.

"Darn," Stuart sighed. "I love Pez."

"How about the Klez Marvels?!" Royce suggested, his mind half on music and half on comic books.

"Maybe," Benny said. "Or we could call ourselves the Freylekh Four."

"No!" the others shouted.

"It's too close to the Neanderthal Four," Jennifer said.

Benny looked at the group reflected in the window.

115

There he was—a tall, thin pinball master with a brown fedora resting atop his curly hair. Royce wore a lime-green bow tie and an Incredible Hulk T-shirt while he practiced a Brahms clarinet sonata. Stuart chewed a wad of gum so massive he looked like he belonged on the pitcher's mound at Yankee Stadium. Jennifer had a Thelonious Monk button pinned to her blue-jeans jacket. He smiled.

"I've got it!" Benny said. "We're the Klez Misfits! Like the Island of Misfit Toys in the Rudolph the Red-Nosed Reindeer show. Get it?"

The band let the name sink in.

Jennifer spoke first. "B-Man, you're a genius! A misfit … and a genius!"

"Sounds good to me," Royce said. "So what does everyone think? Is our new name the Klez Misfits?"

"Onward, forward, and upward as the Klez Misfits!" Stuart shouted.

Over the next hour of practice, all the Klez Misfits added their own personal inspirations to the band's sound—a touch of jazz from Jennifer, classical virtuosity from Royce, a bit of Cajun from Stuart, and the klezmer vibe filling Benny's soul.

"I believe we're ready, except for one thing," Benny said.

"What's that?" Jennifer asked.

"An encore. I'm pretty sure we're going to need one."

≥ ♪ ≤

Walking home from Alistair's Oddities, Benny found it hard to believe he was considering an encore—even *more* time in front of an audience. He thought back to his first violin lesson. His parents and Uncle Maxwell had hoped music might bring him out of the funk he had been in since the Sabbath play.

While Benny loved hearing Uncle Maxwell fiddle, he had serious doubts about trying the violin himself. Playing an instrument meant performing. It meant getting on stage. In Benny's mind, it meant being laughed at.

The sights and sounds in Uncle Maxwell's apartment usually thrilled Benny. On the day of that first lesson, though, he would have much rather been at home reading an X-Men comic book.

"Hey, my little man," Uncle Maxwell had said. "Here's something special just for you." He handed Benny a violin case. "Go ahead, open it. It was my first violin when I was your age. The perfect size to get you started."

Inside rested a half-size violin and a bow. In a compartment at one end Benny found a chunk of rosin and extra strings coiled in a loop. Benny touched the fiddle's ornate scroll, peeked through its f-holes, and ran his fingers over the thin, deep-brown wood making up its body. He held it close to his chest for several minutes as if protecting it from harm.

"May I try it?"

"Be my guest."

Benny placed the fiddle under his chin and, like a

toddler gripping a spoon, clutched the end of the bow in his right hand. He dragged it across the G string, emitting the sound of a creaking door opening in a haunted house. Uncle Maxwell heard something different: the sweet sound of a new beginning.

"I know you'll take good care of it," Uncle Maxwell said at the end of the lesson.

"I will. Thank you," Benny said.

"You are more than welcome." Uncle Maxwell gave him a hug.

Before leaving, Benny looked down at the case and frowned.

"Is something wrong? You like the fiddle, yes?"

Benny nodded. "Yes, I like it, but will I ever have to play for anyone? Can it be a secret?"

"You can play for whoever you want. And we can keep this a secret for as long as you wish."

♪ **16** ♪

The next day before the first bell rang, Benny stood in front of his locker, staring at a sign glued to its front. Royce shook his head in disgust. Jennifer looked like she was ready to punch a hole through the metal door.

"Jason's gone too far this time," Jennifer said.

The sign showed the photograph of Benny from the pinball tournament, the one Sam mentioned at breakfast. The words "BENNY GOES BUST!" had been crossed out. In their place someone had written in purple ink, "BENNY EXPLODES AT THE TALENT SHOW!" Through computer manipulation, Benny's face had been cast in a grape-colored hue.

In the rush of students moving down the hallway, Benny heard bursts of laughter and familiar insults.

"Why would somebody do this?" he asked, kicking the bottom of his locker.

"I'm sure it's Jason," Royce said. "It has to be. I've read

enough comic books to recognize the work of a villain. I bet he's trying to get you to drop out of the show."

"He's probably still mad at you for making him sweat at the pinball tournament," Jennifer said.

"Should we tell Principal Dobkins?" Royce asked.

"What good would it do?" Benny said. "And what proof do I have that it was Jason?" Benny also knew that doing so would violate his rule for handling the unexpected: Don't make things worse.

As Benny pulled out a ruler to scrape off the paper, he spotted Ollie down the hallway. He was talking with Jason and the Neanderthals. Ollie reached out and shook Jason's hand before going into his homeroom.

For several days Benny had tried to get in touch with Ollie. Each text, instant message, and phone call went unanswered.

Now he's talking to the Adjudicator himself. Even shook his hand.

"This may not be Jason alone," Benny said. "He could have had help." He gazed down at the shredded paper lying at his feet and saw a friendship ripped to pieces.

≷ ♪ ≶

Lying in bed, Benny was about to hit "send" on a text to Ollie: I know it was you. Instead, he deleted it. Benny could accept that Ollie was no longer a friend … but an enemy?

He remembered the day they met. It was early in the school year during gym class. "We're going to practice cartwheels today," Mr. Mettner, the gym teacher, said. "Form a line and let's get started."

This was a big problem for Benny. Tumbling made him dizzy. He could not understand why it didn't make everyone dizzy, or how anybody, other than circus performers, could enjoy flipping through the air. Or why cartwheels were even considered a necessary part of his education.

Benny stood in front of Ollie at the back of the line. Padded mats stretched halfway down the length of the gym like vinyl-covered planks waiting to send Benny to the circling sharks.

"I need a volunteer to demonstrate a cartwheel," Mr. Mettner said.

Amanda sprang to her feet and bounded to the mats. She performed four perfect cartwheels followed by a forward roll and a backflip. When done, she spread her arms and looked around as if expecting to see an Olympic judge holding up a perfect ten placard from the top bleacher.

"Good job, Amanda! Now let's see the rest of you do three cartwheels in a row." One by one, Benny's classmates sprinted and spun. Some cartwheels were better than others, but at least they all *looked* like cartwheels. Soon only Benny and Ollie remained.

"Can you hold these?" Benny asked Ollie, handing him his glasses.

"Absolutely. Go get 'em."

Benny rushed the mats. His outstretched right hand made contact with the floor but crumpled. He hit the mat chin first, sending his legs sprawling above his head before crashing in a heap. Taunts followed. He pulled himself up and began limping away.

"Not so fast, Feldman. You've got two more cartwheels to go," Mr. Mettner said.

You've got to be kidding! Wasn't that enough humiliation for one day? Now I'll be known as the exploding, cartwheeling grape!

Ollie stepped in before Benny made his second attempt. "Here's your glasses. Watch this."

Ollie charged the mat and tripped over its front edge. He rolled into a rack of volleyballs that dropped like a shower of honeydews onto the gym teacher's head. After two more tries, he spun so out of control that Mr. Mettner blew his whistle to stop the carnage.

For the rest of the day, the entire school talked about Ollie, the new kid who bombed in gym class.

During lunch, Benny brought his tray to the table where Ollie sat.

"Mind if I join you?" he asked.

"Sure, but this is strictly a no-tumbling zone," Ollie grinned.

"Deal."

Benny learned later that Ollie was one of the best gymnasts in the school.

And now he's hanging out with Jason. How is this possible?

♪ **17** ♪

For the Klez Misfits' next practice, the band met at Uncle Maxwell's apartment. "Leave your instruments at home," Benny had instructed them.

"What kind of practice *is* this?" Jennifer whispered as she settled on the sofa.

"You'll see. My uncle has his ways," Benny said.

"Welcome, fellow musicians," Uncle Maxwell said. "I'm glad you all could make it today."

"Benny has told us a lot about you," Jennifer said.

"Oh, Benny, you didn't talk about the kilt. Tell me you didn't mention that."

"Maybe once or twice," Benny said as they all laughed.

Instruments from Uncle Maxwell's travels around the world filled the living room: talking drums from Senegal, a tin whistle from Ireland, a koto from Japan, a bandura from Ukraine, an Alpine zither from Hungary, an Egyptian oud, and a hammered dulcimer from West Virginia.

"This place is a museum," Stuart said.

"Not quite," Uncle Maxwell replied. "Every instrument here is meant to be played, not just looked at and admired."

"Phenomenal!" Royce said, picking up the tin whistle.

Jennifer tried out the African drums and Benny plucked the strings of the zither. Stuart played a concertina with pearl buttons on either side. Uncle Maxwell rocked in his chair, letting the exotic blend of the different sounds transport him back to people and places in his past.

"Okay, guys, let's get down to work," Uncle Maxwell said eventually. He pulled out his fiddle. The instrument had come down through the family from Moshe. Deep scars marked its dark walnut exterior. A carved lion-head scroll at the top was missing its left ear and part of its snout. "Now close your eyes, listen, and feel the music."

After the first few notes, Benny recognized "Kaddisch" by Maurice Ravel. Uncle Maxwell had played this sad melody at his grandparents' funerals after the recitation of the Mourner's Kaddish, the solemn prayer for the dead. The room was silent except for the sound of the lone violin.

Jennifer wiped tears away. Stuart strained to compose himself. Royce put his hands over his face.

With the final note still hanging in the air, Uncle Maxwell asked, "What did this bring to mind?"

"My father," Stuart said. "I don't see him much since the divorce. He stayed in Louisiana and I miss him."

"It reminded me of the first time I saw my mother cry—when my little brother was in the hospital with pneumonia," Royce said.

"Our golden retriever, Isabel," Jennifer said. "She was fourteen when she died last spring."

Benny's eyes turned wet. "Saying goodbye to my grandparents."

"Thanks for sharing your memories," Uncle Maxwell said. "I know remembering can be hard. Let's try this again."

This time he played a lively tune called "Unser Toirele." After a few measures, the sadness in the room lifted and everyone was smiling. With a final sweep of the bow, the piece ended and the group clapped.

"Thank you. Thank you. That's always been one of my favorites. So what did the music make you think of?"

"Playing dodgeball in the street with Dad and the neighborhood kids," Stuart said.

Royce grinned. "The day my brother came home from the hospital and opened his birthday presents."

"Running with Isabel at the dog park," Jennifer said.

Benny choked back happier tears. "My grandparents dancing the hora at my cousin's bar mitzvah."

"Such wonderful memories," Uncle Maxwell said, pulling a quarter from his vest pocket and flipping it in the air. "Here's one coin, two sides. One side represents joy, the other, sorrow. Klezmer musicians—actually all true musicians—know both sides well. The emotions expressed through their music are relatable for everyone. Everyone who laughs. Everyone who grieves. Everyone who lives."

Before the band left, Uncle Maxwell slipped the coin into Benny's shirt pocket. "This is for you to keep ... to help you remember."

On the car ride home, Jennifer held Benny's hand. "I like your uncle ... and you."

"I like you, too," Benny said, his internal coin flipping to joy.

♪

Holding the quarter, Benny looked at the photograph of Moshe and imagined him telling one of Uncle Maxwell's most familiar stories about his great-grandfather.

It was December 1906, a Russian winter so cold it made a fiddler's hands cry for mercy. Winter is a lean time for a klezmer musician. There were moments when, weakened in body and spirit by the brutal cold, Minna and I looked at my fiddle and wondered if it would be better used for kindling to keep our fire lit. We struggled to put food on the table to feed our small family. But somehow we managed.

We had been blessed with a beautiful son who had grown into a tall, handsome young man with black curly hair and the beginnings of a beard. (At this part of the story, Uncle Maxwell always interjected, "That was my grandfather, Boris.")

Boris was an eager student, more than willing to listen to all my memories about life as a musician. It didn't take long for him to surpass me as a klezmer fiddler. Such a sweet vibrato wept from his instrument that you would have thought all the world's sorrow flowed from him alone. And when we celebrated in our tiny house, Boris played as if all the laughter in the universe had chosen to reside in the hollow of his fiddle.

Boris was a joy in our lives, but Minna and I knew it would be greedy for us to keep such a source of light in such a dark place. In our village, life had become unbearable for Jews. We only wanted to live in peace but were constantly in fear for our lives.

So Minna and I made a decision. On Boris's eighteenth birthday, we handed him money to buy a ticket to America. It was almost all we had.

"Will I go without you?" Boris asked.

"Yes. There is not enough money for all of us. We will join you as soon as we are able."

"Then I am staying here."

"No. This is how it must be. You could be conscripted into the army at any moment. We raised you to hold a fiddle, not a rifle."

After Boris set sail from Nikolaev, we cried for months, fearing we would never see our precious son again. Never hear him play his fiddle. Never have him by our side as we grew old. But with every letter and photograph he sent us—his first apartment, his bride, his newborn son—we rejoiced, knowing he was safe. It would be many years before we saw him again.

But whenever I played my fiddle, Boris was in my heart, a heart split down the middle between sadness and happiness.

♫ **18** ♫

Benny sat by his father's desk at the *Ardmore Star*, the local daily paper. The day's edition had been "put to bed," meaning the stories had been edited, headlines written, and the presses were rolling. By morning, rubber-banded copies filled with grocery coupons and articles about corrupt politicians would be tossed on front porches all over town. Sleeves rolled up, Mr. Feldman leaned back in his swivel chair and sipped from a mug of coffee.

"So, what's the news, Benny?" he asked.

Benny felt funny burdening his father with his troubles. Mr. Feldman spent the day working on stories about labor strikes, violent criminals, car accidents, and polluted rivers. Benny's worries sounded small in comparison. But his father always listened as if his son's sixth-grade dramas deserved a huge headline on page one.

"I'm not sure where to begin," Benny said.

"Just give me the lead." This was a game his father played. He told Benny once that a good reporter could condense all the Harry Potter books into a single paragraph. As an editor, he enjoyed getting right to the meat of a story.

Benny thought for a moment and spoke in his best news anchor voice: "Eleven-year-old Benny Feldman of Ardmore, Ohio, formed a klezmer band, gained a girlfriend, almost won a pinball tournament, and lost his best friend, who may have vandalized his locker and joined forces with Jason the Adjudicator."

"Nicely done! You've got my attention. Now fill in the details."

Mr. Feldman listened as Benny hit the high and low points of the past few weeks. When Benny paused, his father's newspaper instincts took over and he began questioning his son like he would the mayor or chief of police: "Why didn't you tell the principal? Any suspects other than Jason and Ollie? Tell me more about Jennifer. Hand-holding, huh? Still haven't made up with Jason after all this time?"

"No, Jason still bugs me when he gets the chance."

"Why?"

"It doesn't make sense, Dad. He's super-popular. All the girls like him. He's a great guitarist and his band rocks. He has everything!"

Benny glanced at his dad and noticed his tired eyes. They usually appeared this way after a day in front of a computer screen at the office. His father returned the look with a patient smile. Later they would go home together and share a bowl of buttered popcorn while watching an old Godzilla movie on cable. On Monday he would drop off Benny in front of the school and, as he always did, kiss him on the forehead and say, "See you later, newsmaker."

He has everything. Benny looked again at his father and blushed. In his mind he saw Jason reading his personal essay about his father stationed thousands of miles away.

"Okay, not *everything*," Benny said. "But I still don't like how he treats me. I wish he would leave me alone."

"Have you talked with him?"

"I tried. Didn't work."

"What did he say?"

"That he would steamroll us at the talent show."

Mr. Feldman pointed to a stack of newspapers on the corner of his desk. "What do you see?"

"More Hanukkah wrapping paper for Uncle Maxwell?"

"Probably. But what else?"

"Just a bunch of old newspapers."

"Correct. All filled with yesterday's news."

Benny understood his father's point, but he also knew that Jason wasn't letting him—or anyone—forget his past.

"I know, Dad. But what if the news never changes?"

"Then *you* have to write a new headline."

"Like what?"

"Whatever *you* want it to be."

Looking around the empty newsroom, Benny came up with two words: "Everyone Danced."

♪

The next morning Benny found a second sign glued to his locker. This time the culprit superimposed Benny's yearbook headshot over and over onto a cluster of grapes. Underneath it read, "BENNY'S A LOOSER."

"I see our vandal could use a spelling tutor," Royce said, shaking his head.

"You need to tell someone this time," Jennifer said.

"Still no proof," Benny replied. "Help me scrape this off, would ya?"

Benny looked down the hallway where he had seen Ollie and Jason the first time his locker was defaced. This time he couldn't find any suspects among the bustle of students.

It's going to take more than a couple of signs to make me quit. And nobody calls me a "looser."

♪ 19 ♪

Winter break meant Benny could spend more time with Jennifer. A light snow fell as they walked, holding hands, in the woods behind her house. She was trying out some new jokes on Benny, who would not have minded if she read the dictionary out loud from A to Z.

"Why couldn't Handel pay his bills?

"Don't know."

"Because he was baroque."

"How do you repair a big brass instrument?"

"Beats me."

"With a tuba glue."

The worse the joke, the louder Jennifer laughed. This made Benny chuckle, causing them both to break out in a fit of giggles that startled a flock of sparrows out of a nearby sycamore tree.

They strolled awhile in silence, alone with their thoughts. Out of the corner of his eye, Benny saw Jennifer's G-clef earrings and the pompom atop her hat. He had never kissed a girl. Willing participants weren't exactly lining up for him. As the light snow covered his fedora, he wondered if he was doing the "boyfriend" thing correctly. He had even switched from watching monster movies to romantic comedies to give him clues on how to act. It didn't help.

Give me a page of notes to play and I'll find my way to the end just fine. Put me in the woods with a girl I like and I'm lost, wandering off course without a compass.

Unsure of what to do next, Benny defaulted to his comfort zone—rambling on about klezmer.

"I have some ideas for the band's encore," he said in a rush of words. "At first I was sure we'd perform 'Dyadushka Polka.' It would give Royce a great chance to shine. He's getting better and better at making his clarinet laugh and cry. That's called *dreydlekh*."

Jennifer nodded as Benny charged on.

"Then I thought, no, let's try 'The Happy Nigun.' *Nigun* means melody. What better way to end our performance than with a happy melody? Who wouldn't dance to that? Then I started looking through all my music books and changed my mind."

"Benny?"

"That's when I found a tune that would be perfect for Stuart. And it has a sweet spot for a drum solo. It's really catchy."

"Benny?"

"Maybe we could string three short tunes together. That'd be crazy. Let's see: We'll start with—"

"BENNY!" Jennifer stopped and let go of his hand. "There's something I need to talk with you about."

"Sorry, I got carried away."

"I spoke with my parents about being in the Klez Misfits' performance."

Benny detected a hint of uncertainty in Jennifer's voice. "Is there a problem?"

"Oh, no. Dad is totally cool with it. He's drummed at Jewish weddings before and says they're a blast."

"And your mom?"

"She's excited about it, too. She even suggested a song for us to play."

"She suggested a song?"

"My mom thought 'Bei Mir Bistu Shein' might make a good encore."

Benny knew the song well. It originated in the Yiddish theater in the 1930s. Later the lyrics were changed and the melody jazzed up. The Andrews Sisters' version done in English became a huge hit. It was *not at all* what Benny had in mind.

"That song is popular, but there are so many others," he said.

"I found out it was my grandmother's favorite. She used to sing it to Mom before bed. It would mean a lot to my mother if we performed it."

"There's a big problem. The Klez Misfits don't have a singer."

"Yes we do."

"Who?"

"Me," Jennifer said, pointing to herself. "I've learned the song and I'm practicing the chorus in Yiddish."

"You'd do that?"

"Yes, B-Man."

Kiss her now, Benny thought. He stood frozen. He had never come up with a rule for what to do in this situation. So he went back to talking about the band.

"Klezmer must be part of your DNA, too. No wonder you joined the band the first day we met."

"Not quite. At first I joined because Jason was picking on you. I hate bullies like him."

"You felt sorry for me?" Benny turned away. He did not like being an object of pity.

"Not sorry. Angry. You needed someone to stand up for you. That's why I stepped in."

"What about now?"

"Now it's about the music. It's about the band. And it's about you." Jennifer kissed Benny on the cheek.

"Did you know that 'Bei Mir Bistu Shein' means 'to me you are beautiful'?" Benny asked. He leaned in and kissed her cheek.

They stood beneath the frosted branches of a willow tree—two figures encased in a private snow globe in the middle of the woods.

♪

After Benny had played his scales and exercises, Uncle Maxwell asked him what klezmer tune he would like to play for dessert. "'Tantz, Tantz Yiddelech,' I assume?"

"No, I'd like to practice 'Bei Mir Bistu Shein.' It may be our encore. Jennifer said she would sing it."

Benny didn't mind the song's corny English lyrics about a lonely girl who finds her true love. And he thought having the chorus sung in Yiddish would give it some klezmer cred. But in his heart Benny still felt the song wasn't right for the band. He wanted something more traditional. Something Moshe might have played.

"An excellent choice!" Uncle Maxwell said, slapping his hands on his knees.

Benny was surprised. He thought Uncle Maxwell would share his skepticism about the selection.

"It's just too popular," Benny said. "I know it swings, but I'm having a little trouble with it."

"There's nothing wrong with popular," Uncle Maxwell said. "Listen, imagine it's 1937. People all over the country are turning on their radios. And what do they hear? The words 'Bei Mir Bistu Shein.' When they go out to the clubs, what are they dancing to? 'Bei Mir Bistu Shein.' Most of them don't even know the words are Yiddish, but they've become a part of their lives. I've played the song often. It never fails to bring down the house."

Benny listened but wasn't entirely convinced.

"Also, did you know the song's title was translated into

German and it became a hit in Nazi Germany?" Uncle Maxwell asked.

"Really?" Benny wondered how this tidbit of musical lore had escaped him.

"They didn't know 'Bei Mir Bistu Shein' had Jewish roots. So there it was, being sung *in Nazi Germany*. Once the song's origins were discovered, it was banned immediately from the country. Wiped out. Eliminated."

"I didn't know."

"But now, almost eighty years later, the song survives. You tell Jennifer to sing it with all her heart."

"I will."

≩ ♫ ≨

Benny: We have an encore! I emailed you a link to the song.

Royce: Hey, I've heard this on a commercial.

Stuart: It plays in the background of one of my video games.

Jennifer: Thx.

Benny: It's happening next practice. Be ready.

≩ ♫ ≨

In the back of Alistair's Oddities, Jennifer fidgeted behind her drum kit. She had not told a single joke since practice began. Her drum fills lacked their usual in-your-face bluster, and her hits on the high-hat were half-hearted at best. She tossed her drumsticks to the floor and drifted off to the pinball machine.

"Care for a game?" Benny asked, doubting if pinball was on her mind.

"I told Mom I would be singing 'Bei Mir Bistu Shein' at the talent show."

"What did she say?"

"Something awful. She hugged me and said my grandmother would have been so proud."

"Am I missing something? Why is that awful?"

Jennifer didn't respond right away, but Benny recognized the look on her face. It was fear.

"Playing in the back of the band is one thing. But the more I think about singing out in front, the more it freaks me out. I'm waking up at night worrying."

Worrying was a subject Benny understood well. The idea of fiddling in front of a crowd was making him lose more than a few hours of sleep, too.

Having one person in the band with stage fright could send us crashing down in flames. Having two people with stage fright doubles our chances of disaster.

"I guess we were meant for each other," he said.

"Hey, are we going to practice the encore or not?" Stuart shouted as he strapped on his accordion.

"Come on, you two," Royce said. "I didn't practice this tune for nothing. I watched eight different versions of the song, one done by Ella Fitzgerald and another by the

Jackson Five." He started singing in a Michael Jackson falsetto that made Stuart spit out his gum laughing.

Jennifer let out a nervous giggle.

"You can't possibly sound worse than that," Benny said.

Stuart played the song's introduction. Jennifer began snapping her fingers in four-four time and launched into the lyrics, imagining she was the girl in the song and Benny was the boy who made her heart as light as a feather. Benny beamed when Jennifer reached the chorus and sang "Bei mir bistu shein" and belted out other Yiddish words—*kheyn* (charming), *velt* (world), *gelt* (money), and *tayer* (precious)—that would have made Moshe proud.

While Benny and Royce added improvised solos, Jennifer tapped along on her snare. Her voice grew stronger and more confident as the song went along. Drawn by the music, shoppers gathered around the band. When the song ended, a few people dropped dollar bills into Benny's open violin case.

"Wow! J-Kom, you've got some pipes!" Royce said.

"Thanks. Killer solos," she said.

"When is your next gig?" a woman asked.

"The Klez Misfits will be at the Sieberling School talent show on March 15," Alistair said.

"Bring everyone you know," Benny added. "And be sure to ask for an encore."

When the crowd dispersed, only a short woman with red hair remained. She approached Benny. "Thank you," she said.

"I'm glad you enjoyed the music."

"No, I mean thank you for making my son Stuart a part of this. It means so much to me to see him happy again."

Benny glanced over at Stuart, who was playing on the pinball machine with Royce and Jennifer. "You'll be coming to the talent show?" he asked.

"With my dancing shoes on," she replied.

♫ **20** ♫

On the last night of winter break, the word "LOOSER" crept back into Benny's thoughts. He wondered if another sign would be plastered on his locker.

Why so glum, boychick? he imagined Moshe saying. *You got the girl. You got the band. Nice parents. A roof over your head. For better or for worse, the rest will work itself out.*

"I know, I know. But I've got this nagging feeling about the talent show. We all love what we're playing, but what if nobody else does?"

Listen to me and your Uncle Maxwell. By now our family's main rule of survival should be imprinted on your forehead: STOP WORRYING SO MUCH!

Stop worrying so much. Benny had heard it countless times from his parents.

"You don't understand. How long has it been since you were in sixth grade?" Benny said.

Worry is worry, no matter how old you are. Let me tell you, as a traveling klezmer musician, I stood near the bottom of the social ladder. Everyone wanted me to play at their weddings and brisses, but otherwise I was looked down upon. Ridiculed. Mocked.

"Didn't that bother you?"

When you're trying to survive from one day to the next, there's little time for such foolishness. Love me. Hate me. Ignore me. That's their problem, not mine. Not everyone is going to like you, Benny. And if they do, let me tell you, you're doing something wrong.

"Well, I guess that means I must be doing something right," Benny sighed.

♪ 21 ♪

The sixth-graders in Room 610 huddled around an open laptop on Jason's desk. Amanda pushed her way through to get a good look. Ms. Krumholtz was nowhere in sight, having escorted Liam Bledsole to the nurse's office with his fourth nosebleed that year.

"And now, the world premiere of the Neanderthal Four's new video!" Jason said, performing a drum roll with his hands on his notebook. "Dad bought me studio time as a Hanukkah present so I could record my band's latest song, 'Run for Your Caves.'"

Amanda smiled, noting that the video only had twenty-seven views. "Mine has 112,456," she muttered, punching numbers on her phone's calculator. "That's 112,429 more than Jason's."

Benny tried to resist, but he turned his head to get an unobstructed view of the screen. The video began with Jason emerging through a thick fog, holding his Flying V guitar. An off-screen wind machine blew his hair. The camera zoomed in, showing his left hand fingering the top frets, then sliding down to an E minor power chord that ended with fireworks exploding behind the gigantic speakers. Sticks McCracken on the drums thundered in the background. Filbert Jones's throbbing bass and Theresa Charleton's cascading synthesizer added to the growing frenzy.

Jason grabbed the microphone and screamed:

> No one can touch us!
> Guess what's in store!
> Better watch out for
> The Neanderthal Four!
>
> We're coming for you!
> Get out of our way!
> We'll turn your blue skies
> To a new shade of gray!
>
> So hide in your caves
> Or run for the door.
> You won't ever forget
> The Neanderthal Four!

Students bobbed their heads to the thrashing beat and played along on air guitars. The noise hurt Benny's temples. The Neanderthal Four were loud, twenty times louder than the Klez Misfits. *And all the members are popular in school, a thousand times more popular than us,* Benny thought. The video ended with a close-up of Jason. Without instrumental backup, he sang:

> Destiny nears.
> We know the score.
> Hail to the champs—
> The Neanderthal Four!

The screen faded to darkness. The class cheered and pumped their fists. Jason's video made Benny feel small, like David brandishing a fiddle against Goliath and a Flying V guitar.

"That's not all," Jason said as he opened a folder and pulled out a pencil sketch. "Check out my band's new logo."

Benny recognized Ollie's artistic style. He shrunk back in his chair.

Ollie made a logo for Jason! The semester is only ten minutes old and already spinning out of control.

Ms. Krumholtz returned, scowling. "Benny. Jason. Principal Dobkins wants to see you both in his office. Immediately."

Stop worrying so much? Maybe I'll start that tomorrow.

≩ ♪ ≧

The boys sat side by side on hard chairs facing Principal Dobkins' desk.

Benny had been called to the principal's office only once before. In third grade he accidently left a tuna fish sandwich in his locker over spring break. Even with blasts of disinfectant spray, the smell lingered for days.

Jason and Principal Dobkins had been well acquainted since kindergarten. Jason's list of infractions included everything from sleeping in class to getting an after-school detention for plugging in his Flying V guitar and playing it during homeroom.

"Feldman, Conroy, follow me." Principal Dobkins led them to the cafeteria. Written in large purple letters across several tables were the words, "KLEZMIR RULES! NEANDERTHALS STINK!"

The sight of the vandalized lunch tables rattled Benny. His former main rule for avoiding trouble at school, "Blend into the background," had been broken repeatedly since he signed up for the talent show. Now he was suspected of a crime that could get him suspended.

"You two realize this violates Section 3.4 of the Student Responsibility Code forbidding graffiti on school property."

"I didn't do this," Benny said.

"Liar! Yes, you did!" Jason said.

"No, you did it to get me in trouble!"

"You're just jealous because the Neanderthal Four are going to obliterate you!"

"Dream on!" Benny flashed back to first grade and his last extended debate with Jason about grapes versus bread.

"No, *you* dream on!" Jason said.

"That's enough!" Principal Dobkins said. "Now, go ask the custodian for buckets, soap, and rags to clean up this mess. When I come back in half an hour, I want these tables spotless. And if there's even a whiff of trouble from either of you, you're both out of the talent show *and* suspended for a full week."

Benny and Jason cleaned the tables in silence. With a little elbow grease, the inky words disappeared. Benny wished it was this easy to erase the way Jason had treated him.

As Benny scrubbed away, he tried to write a new headline: Old Friends Make Peace.

"Your father gave you a great Hanukkah gift," Benny said.

Jason ignored him, gathered up his cleaning supplies, and walked away.

≥ ♪ ≤

Before practice, Benny showed Jason's video to the Klez Misfits. He expected an all-out mutiny by the band. In light of the Neanderthal Four's impressive display, he imagined they would lay down their instruments and call it quits.

"Hmmm, not very lyrically deep," Royce said, shrugging. "It sounds like a one-sided rap battle but with weaker lyrics. 'So hide in your caves?' That's V-A-P-I-D."

"Meh," Jennifer said. "Lots of rage, not a bit of joy."

"Admit it, though. They're good musicians," Benny said.

"Yes, and so are we," Stuart declared. "Besides, they don't have our secret weapon—MY ACCORDION!" He hoisted his instrument above his head.

"Maybe we should get ourselves a wind machine," Royce said.

"We already have one," Jennifer joked, pointing at Stuart.

"I'm serious, guys," Benny said. "You should have seen my homeroom jamming to their music. How can we compete against that?"

"Are you going to back out?" Royce asked. "That's not an option. I just bought the perfect gold tie for the talent show, and I plan on wearing it."

"What's up, B-Man? It can't be this video. What's really bothering you?" Jennifer asked.

"Somebody vandalized the cafeteria tables to make it look like I did it," he said. "Principal Dobkins warned me if anything else happens, I'm out of the talent show and suspended from school. I'm sorry I dragged you all into this *meshugas*."

"*Meshugas*? That sounds like a disease. Should I be worried?" Stuart asked.

"No, it's Yiddish for craziness," Benny said.

"Listen, Benny, without you, there *is* no band. If you're quitting, I'm out, too," Royce said.

"I'm not quitting. I'm … I'm…."

"Scared about playing in front of the entire school?" Jennifer said.

Benny swallowed hard. "Terrified."

"Join the club," Jennifer said.

♪ 22 ♪

Benny turned Moshe's photograph to the wall so he could concentrate on figuring out who was behind the trouble at school. He wrote down a list of suspects:

Ollie
- Former friend turned enemy
- Designed a logo for Jason
- Won't return texts
- Not a good speller.

Jason
- Hates losing
- Capable of doing anything to make me look bad
- Wants the Klez Misfits out of the talent show.

Sticks, Filbert, or Theresa
- Members of the Neanderthal Four helping out Jason.

The more Benny stared at the list, the more paranoid he became. *Maybe it's Sam. He was the one who found the "Benny Goes Bust" photo online. What about that kid who tried to play "Yankee Doodle" on the recorder? Could Amanda still be mad at me for beating her at pinball? Is Ms. Krumholtz a CIA agent? Alistair an evil alien robot?*

Benny's head spun as he examined the possibilities. The talent show was only two weeks away. Petrified or not, he owed it to the Klez Misfits to perform. He owed it to all those who supported him: his parents, Uncle Maxwell, Alistair, and Cantor Berkowitz. And he owed it to Moshe.

If I don't try, I'll be known as the Amazing Exploding Grape. Forever.

His mother knocked on his bedroom door. "Ollie is downstairs. He says he has to tell you something."

Benny turned Moshe's picture back around. "Any thoughts?"

You're on your own with this one, boychick.

≳ ♫ ≲

Benny wasted no time. He walked straight to Ollie and demanded answers. "Admit it!" he said, towering over Ollie. "You glued those signs to my locker and wrote on the cafeteria tables!"

Ollie remained calm. "No, Benny, I didn't."

"Did your new pal Jason put you up to it?"

"No, I swear. And Jason's not my pal."

"Then who did it?"

"I have no idea."

"Then why are you here?"

"Maybe I shouldn't have come."

"Maybe you shouldn't have."

Ollie turned to leave. Benny spoke before he reached the door.

"Don't lie. I saw you talking with Jason. I saw you shake his hand."

Ollie wheeled around. "Jason paid me to design a new logo for his band. I didn't volunteer. He came to me. It was business. That's all."

"So that's your confession? That's what you came here to tell me?" Benny shook with anger. Ollie stood his ground.

"No."

"Then *what*? What is it?"

"Dude, I miss hanging out with you."

Ollie's words felt like a bucket of cold water splashing across Benny's face. He took a deep breath and recalled what Ollie had told him months before: "You have me. That's not going to change." Benny remembered what it felt like when Jason stopped being his friend.

"I miss hanging out with you, too. I'm sorry I ignored you at the convention. All I've been thinking about is winning the talent show."

"I'm sorry, too," Ollie said. "I felt left out. I know this

performance is important to you." Ollie reached out and bumped fists with Benny.

"Friends?" Ollie said.

"Friends," Benny answered. "And, by the way, your logo for Jason's band is sweet."

"Thanks. I was hoping you'd let me design a logo for Benny Feldman's All-Star Klezmer Band. No charge."

"We're now called the Klez Misfits. And yes, a logo would be great!"

"You got it."

"Our next practice is Saturday at Alistair's. Hope you can make it."

After Ollie departed, Benny crossed his name off the list of suspects and texted Jennifer.

Ollie is back.

So it wasn't him?

No.

I bet Jason's our guy. Case closed.

♪ 23 ♪

The Klez Misfits grew more confident playing together with each practice.

"Now you're listening to each other!" Alistair said, twirling a dressmaker's dummy around the shop floor as the band played.

With only one week left until the talent show, the band had taken complete command of "Tantz, Tantz Yiddelech." They could shift tempos and change dynamics from thundering to whispering in a heartbeat. Royce could now make his clarinet go "yuck-yuck-yuck" as if laughing at one of Jennifer's jokes. They worked in a part where the fiddle and accordion responded back and forth. When the tune reached top speed, the band stopped and shouted "HEY!" together as loud as they could.

For the encore, Jennifer moved in front of the band and played a fast four-four beat on her snare drum to kick off "Bei Mir Bistu Shein." The Yiddish chorus rolled off her tongue.

Hearing the catchy music drift into the street, people came into Alistair's Oddities and clapped along to the beat. Then they stayed to check out the shop's quirky offerings.

"I'm not going to lie," Alistair confided to Benny during a break. "Thanks to you guys, this has been my biggest sales month since the place opened. To help out the band, I made these fliers." He gave one to Benny.

SWING TO THE KRAZIEST KLEZMER BAND IN TOWN!
See the Klez Misfits LIVE!!!
Sieberling School Talent Show
March 15, 7:00 p.m.
1512 Peony Lane

"I've handed these out to all my customers and posted it on my website. Check out the stack by the cash register and the one in the front window."

"You ... are ... the ... best!" Benny said.

Benny looked around the shop. Ollie was drawing in his sketchpad. Stuart blew an enormous bubble that burst across his face. Royce tried pedaling an old unicycle down the center aisle. Jennifer giggled out loud as she read from a joke book.

He thought about his long list of rules for getting through the day. *Maybe it's time for a new one: Enjoy the ride.*

♫ **24** ♫

Benny overheard his mother talking on the phone with his Aunt Esther. He could tell the Klez Misfits were the main topic of their conversation. Pacing the floor, he waited for her to hang up.

"Did you invite Aunt Esther and Uncle Fred to the talent show?"

"Hey, I do the cross-examinations around here."

"Mom, who else did you invite?" Benny was ready to "enjoy the ride." He just didn't anticipate that so many people would be joining him in the back seat.

"A few friends and relatives."

Benny understood this to mean the entire family tree, from Uncle Maxwell to third cousins he had not seen since his consecration.

"Sara and Jordan, too?" His cousins had attended the Sunday school play and never failed to mention the debacle, especially when grape juice was being poured during the Passover seder. Benny always imagined which plague would suit them best. Frogs usually topped the list.

"Yes, I invited them. And for the sake of argument, when you asked me *not* to let anyone know, it was because at that time you didn't have a full band. Now you do."

"You're right, but did you have to tell *everyone* about it?"

"Benny, this is your chance to share your talent. It's also a chance to rewrite the past. Not everyone gets that opportunity."

Benny couldn't refute his mother's words. He only worried that once the chapter got rewritten, the ending would be even worse.

♫ 25 ♫

As the day of the talent show approached, Benny's fingers felt stiff and awkward. His bowing arm seemed weighed down as if a hippopotamus perched on his right elbow.

"Relax," Royce said. "Remember what your Uncle Maxwell told us: Feel the music and forget about everything else."

Benny tried, but all he could think about were the hot lights. The stage. The crowd. The Neanderthal Four.

Ollie entered Alistair's Oddities carrying a brown box.

"OOOLLLIIIEEE!" Alistair said. "Pull up a chair and sit a spell."

"I can't stay long. I wanted to drop off these for the band. Check this out."

Ollie held up a black T-shirt with a comic-book-style drawing of the Klez Misfits dressed as superheroes. Jennifer had lightning bolts shooting from her drumsticks. Stuart looked like a Transformer with his accordion embedded in a robotic body. Benny's fiddle was made of fire, and silver violin bows filled a quiver strapped to his back. Royce wore a powdered Mozart wig, flowing cape, green mask, and matching bow tie.

"You offered to do a logo, but this … this…." Benny stammered.

"It's my gift to all of you," Ollie said, handing each a Klez Misfits T-shirt. "My dad helped out. He runs a screen-printing shop."

"Could you take a picture of the band?" Jennifer asked, handing her phone to Alistair. "I'd like to post it online."

The Klez Misfits struck a pose wearing the T-shirts and holding their instruments. Ollie stood off to one side.

"Hey, O-Leaf. Get over here," Jennifer said.

"Nah, this shoot is for band members only."

"Enough with the M-E-L-O-D-R-A-M-A," Royce said. "You *are* part of the band."

"Absolutely!" Stuart said.

"Alright." Ollie stood next to Benny and grinned as Alistair took the band's first official group shot.

They clustered around to inspect the photo.

"Time for a riddle," Jennifer said.

"Nooooo!" they all groaned.

"What has a puffy cheek, a fedora, bow tie, red horn-rimmed glasses, and a friend who can really draw?"

"The Klez Misfits!" they said as one.

≷ ♫ ≷

The next day, Benny, Jennifer, Royce, and Ollie wore their band T-shirts to school. For the first time, students congregated around Benny's desk in homeroom. They agreed that the Klez Misfits' logo was better than the Neanderthal Four's—a Tyrannosaurus Rex chomping a Flying V guitar. But they also agreed that a logo wouldn't stop Jason's band from chomping them to bits at the talent show.

Amanda glanced at Benny's shirt and frowned. Jason remained quiet.

"Settle down, class. Everyone in your seats," Ms. Krumholtz said. "It's time for the morning announcements."

Benny smiled. He knew that it was *not* going to be a typical day at Sieberling School. And that was fine with him. *Not* typical meant you might meet a girl who played a mean drum solo or make friends with a clarinet prodigy wearing a Wolverine T-shirt.

"For those participating in the talent show, the school will be open early tomorrow so you can bring whatever equipment you'll need to perform," Ms. Krumholtz said. "And all the participants must meet in the auditorium at noon—no exceptions!"

≳ ♪ ≲

During lunch, the twenty talent show acts came to the auditorium to pick numbers to determine the order of the performances. "All spots are final," Principal Dobkins said. "No trading positions. That's the rule."

Sam pulled the number two. Amanda picked seventeen. Jason unfolded a paper with nineteen.

Benny hoped for a low number like a four or five, not the first but not near the end. If he had to wait all evening to play, he feared his nerves would give out. He looked down at the slip in the palm of his hand. "Twenty," he sighed, showing it to Royce and Jennifer.

"Ah, saving the worst for last. *And* you have to follow us. This is P-E-R-F-E-C-T," Jason said, looking at Royce.

Jennifer's face turned the color of her glasses. She strode up to Jason and hovered over him. "I knew kids like you at my old school. Well, you can't hurt me. Or Benny. Or Royce. Or Stuart. Not now! Not ever!"

She stomped out of the auditorium with Benny and Royce following.

"Way to go, J-Kom!" Royce said. "My feelings E-X-A-C-T-L-Y!"

"That's right! Come Thursday night, we're going to kick some Neanderthal *tuchas*!" Benny said.

♫ 26 ♫

Benny climbed into his father's car for the ride home.

"So what's the news, Benny?"

When Benny started to answer, he felt a slight tickle in the back of his throat.

Are you kidding me? This can't be happening. Not the day before the show.

"Something wrong?" Mr. Feldman asked.

"Everything's fine. It's all good," he lied, remembering how his first-grade tickle had morphed into a nightmare.

By the time Benny threw his backpack inside the front door, his throat hurt when he swallowed. He texted Jennifer.

Emergency! Sore throat!

r u sure it's not allergies?

Positive! Help!

Gargle with saltwater! NOW!

Benny ran into the kitchen, stirred a heaping spoonful

of table salt into a glass of warm water, and gargled. Gagging, he spit it out in the sink.

"Benny, what are you doing?" Mr. Feldman asked.

"I have a sore throat … that leads to a head cold … and the show is tomorrow … that means I'm going to hurl onstage…."

"Could it be allergies?"

"NOOOOOO!"

"Calm down. Go upstairs and I'll bring you a bowl of chicken soup. My bubbe always said, 'Nothing knocks out a cold quicker than chicken soup.'"

Benny collapsed on his bed and threw the blankets over his head. He had heard the same line about the wonders of chicken soup for years. It *never* worked. In his mind it was like saying, "Nothing mends a broken arm like a nice warm flannel shirt." But with so much at stake, he was willing to try anything.

Mr. Feldman appeared with soup, crackers, orange slices, and a box of tissues. Having watched his Uncle Maxwell make homemade chicken soup using Moshe's recipe, Benny knew his father's out-of-the-can attempt would displease his great-great-grandfather.

Chicken soup from a tin can? How is that supposed to work? Where's the chicken feet? The rutabagas? The parsnips? The carrots?

Even so, Benny downed the soup and licked the bowl clean. He sucked each orange slice dry, hoping to extract every possible speck of vitamin C.

Benny coughed and sneezed. Desperate, he tried all the folk remedies he knew: inhaling steam in the shower, drinking green tea laced with honey, and working up a good sweat by running in place wearing his winter coat and hat.

Even Moshe had a recommendation. *Fresh horseradish. Nibble a piece of fresh horseradish root. It always worked for me.*

By bedtime, both nostrils were blocked, and Benny's stomach ached from the bitter herb.

"Why now?" he moaned. "How am I going to make it through the school talent show? Ms. Krumholtz will probably introduce me as 'Benny Febman, klebmer fibbler.'"

Benny made a mental list:

The positives: I don't have to dance in a circle wearing a grape costume. Jennifer is handling the singing.

The negatives: I could wobble off stage. Or trip over the drum kit. Or knock Stuart to the ground, where he would rock like a short-circuited Transformer.

The worst-case scenario: What if the Klez Misfits play as if our lives depend on it and nobody likes us anyway?

Benny's final thought gave him a chill: *What if we win and Jason teases us anyway?*

Moshe offered his two cents' worth:

Benny, Benny, Benny. I fiddled my whole life. I must have played a thousand performances—some grand, some not so good. No matter what, I always told myself that if one person—just one person—came away a little happier, a little more at peace, I had done my job. And if I made everyone forget their troubles—even for a moment—I had moved a mountain. Sleep, Benny. Come morning, you'll be ready to move a mountain.

∈ ♫ ∋

Benny's alarm clock blared. He opened his eyes and tried to inhale through his nose. **Miracle of miracles!** he texted Jennifer. **Nasal passages clear! All systems go!**

Great news, B-Man! See you at school around six.

Benny came down to breakfast wearing the band T-shirt, black pants, and fedora. Sam wore a short-sleeved Hawaiian shirt. He juggled two apples, a banana, and a kiwi by the kitchen table.

"So?" Mrs. Feldman said. She had been up half the night imagining Benny would wake up in no condition to fiddle.

"The cold is gone. I feel fine. Nervous but fine."

Relieved, she put her hand to her chest. "It must have been allergies."

"I wasn't worried. That's the power of chicken soup," Mr. Feldman said.

I'm going with the horseradish, Benny thought.

♫ 27 ♫

Mr. Feldman stopped the car by the school's stage door entrance. He put a hand on Benny's shoulder. "Here's today's headline: 'Feldman Parents Proud of Son—No Matter What!'"

Benny smiled. After the Sabbath play fiasco, his parents had praised him for being the best Fruit of the Vine "in a performance no one would ever forget." Sam gushed that his brother was "the best part of the Sabbath play— *by far*." Only later did he learn that Benny's performance had not been part of the script.

"Remember, we love you, Benny. Nothing will ever change that."

"Thanks, Dad. Love you, too," he said. "Gotta go. Jennifer's waiting for me."

With his fiddle case tucked under his arm, Benny walked into the school.

≥ ♪ ≤

Backstage, Jennifer laid out the pieces of her drum kit. Together, she and Benny set up the snare and toms, positioned the bass kick, and screwed in the cymbals. She sat on a swivel stool and practiced warm-up beats as Benny nervously looked out at the rows of empty seats in the auditorium.

From the other side of the stage, Benny spotted Jason and Sticks running toward them. "Come quick," Jason said, panting. "We've got trouble."

"Is this some kind of trick?" Benny asked.

"No! We need to hurry before school starts! Come on!"

Down the long hallway on the first floor, every locker had a sign taped to it showing the photo of the Klez Misfits Jennifer had posted online. A purple X crossed out the band. Underneath it read, "The Exploding Grape Band—Quit or You'll Be Sorry."

"They're all over! Hundreds of them!" Jason said. "And there's a different one plastered everywhere on the second floor. I even saw two signs on Principal Dobkins' door."

"We only have forty-five minutes before the first bell rings," Jennifer said, heading for the stairs. "You and Jason take care of the first floor. Sticks and I will handle the second."

Sticks plucked a sheet off a locker. It showed a screen shot from Jason's video with a headline screaming, "Guitar ZERO Krushed By Klezmir." Jennifer and

Sticks raced down the hall gathering the incriminating signs until each locker was bare.

Benny and Jason flew into restrooms, through the cafeteria, and into classrooms, ripping signs off mirrors, toilets, tables, and desks. They picked up papers scattered on the floor of the art room and gymnasium. Benny snatched down signs covering the bulletin board by the library.

The clock read 6:52. Jason and Benny met Jennifer and Sticks in front of the first-floor girls' restroom. "I'll check in here and then we'll be done." She emerged in a panic. "I need your help! They're plastered all over the walls. I can't do this alone."

"No way am I going in there," Jason said. Sticks nodded.

"I'm with Jason," Benny said. It was the first time they had agreed on anything since kindergarten.

"It's 6:55. Do you want to be in the talent show or not?" Jennifer yelled.

"Not a word to anyone," Jason said, looking around for witnesses before rushing inside. Benny and Sticks followed. In minutes each came out carrying stacks of signs.

The four dropped the papers into a recycling bin just as Principal Dobkins entered the building.

"Well, you're here bright and early. Ready for the talent show?"

Out of breath, all they could do was nod.

"Good. Looking forward to it. I'll be one of the judges," he said.

As Mr. Dobkins turned to leave, they were all struck with a horrifying thought: There were still two signs on the principal's door.

"Gotta go!" Benny said, hustling away with Jason and Sticks trailing close behind.

Stalling, Jennifer blurted out the first thing that popped into her head. "Do you play an instrument, Mr. Dobkins?"

"Funny you should ask. I used to be quite the trumpet player in my younger days. I played a bit of everything—jazz, classical, the blues. In fact, last year I sat in with the school band and played 'Let It Snow.' Such a catchy tune … with a great arrangement."

Down the hall, Jennifer saw Benny, Jason, and Sticks. Benny held up the last remaining sheets.

"Well, I've got to get ready for class. See you tonight!" Jennifer said.

Back in the auditorium, they examined the signs. "These are just like the ones I found glued to my locker," Benny said.

"You had signs on *your* locker? So did I," Jason said. "I was sure you were behind them."

"Somebody is out to get you both," Jennifer said. "But who?"

Benny looked at the purple X crossing out the band's photo and read the line below: "You'll be sorry."

The bell rang.

"Good luck tonight," Benny said to Jason.

"Luck? That's for amateurs like you. We're going to rock your world."

≷ ♪ ≶

During lunch, Benny explained his theory about the signs.

"It's got to be Amanda. She's the only one I know who uses a purple marker. And when I beat her at the pinball tournament, she said to me, 'You'll be sorry.'"

"But why? Why would she do this?" Jennifer asked.

"It's hard to say. Maybe she wants to win that badly," Benny said.

"That's R-E-P-R-E-H-E-N-S-I-B-L-E! Getting rid of the competition before the curtain opens," Royce said, shaking his head.

"Should we blow the whistle on her?" Jennifer asked.

"Now's not the time. And the evidence is still weak. I'm ready to put all of this behind me. Once the talent show is over, my life will go back to normal."

"No it won't," Ollie said.

"What do you mean?" Benny asked.

"After tonight, you'll no longer be known as the Amazing Exploding Grape. You'll be known as Benny Feldman. B-Man. Master Klezmer Fiddler. *That* will be your new normal."

♫ 28 ♫

Before the show, the Klez Misfits gathered around Jennifer's drum kit. To Benny's surprise, they each wore a fedora with different-colored headbands. With Stuart's help, Ollie unfurled a large banner with "THE KLEZ MISFITS" painted in big letters across it.

"Hang this behind the band right before you go on. It's not as good as a wind machine, but it was the best I could do," Ollie said.

"It's better than a wind machine," Benny said, choking up. "Thanks. All of you."

"No thanks necessary," Royce said.

"And here's something for the band," Benny said, handing everyone a sealed white envelope.

"Aw, Benny, you didn't have to. You know we'd have played with you for nothing," Stuart said.

Inside each envelope were coupons good for fifty cents off a combo meal at Frankie's House of Corndogs.

"That's the one right next to Speedy Wash," Benny said.

"Classic!" Royce said.

"You're the corndog, Benny," Stuart laughed.

"What I'm trying to say is *this*: Our playing together— our friendship—doesn't end when the talent show is over. It only begins."

♪ 29 ♪

The lights in the auditorium dimmed. A huge cheer arose as Ms. Krumholtz stepped out from behind the red curtain and addressed the crowd.

"Welcome to the Sieberling School talent show! Our students have worked very hard to prepare and are eager to get started. But before we begin, here's a brief rundown of the rules."

Benny paused from tuning his fiddle for the third time. *Rules? What rules?*

Ms. Krumholtz read off a sheet: "Rule number one: All performers must go in the assigned order. Trading spots is strictly prohibited. Rule number two: All acts will have three minutes to get ready between performances. And lastly, all acts will get five minutes on stage—no exceptions."

"Five minutes!" Jennifer said. "That's only enough time for the first tune. That means no encore! My mom has waited weeks for this."

"I'm so sorry, J-Kom. I didn't know," Benny said. "Maybe we should do 'Bei Mir Bistu Shein' instead. That way you'll get to sing."

"No, absolutely not. 'Tantz, Tantz Yiddelech' highlights all of us. I'll be fine."

But Benny saw the disappointment in her eyes. *How could I have forgotten one of my oldest survival tips?—Know the rules.* His head started throbbing and his stomach grumbled as the first act took their bows.

"Let's give a big hand for Sieberling's own master thespians, Shiver Me Shakespeare. Weren't they wonderful?" Ms. Krumholtz said.

One performance down, eighteen more to go. I'm not going to make it, Benny thought.

≥ ♪ ≤

Standing stage left, Benny gazed at the packed auditorium. The audience was ten times larger than the one at the Sunday school play. Eighth-graders slouched in the first couple of rows, waiting to jeer at the most harmless misstep. Benny saw people from his past scattered throughout the crowd: Karen Neumar, the Grossman twins, and Mrs. Mandelbaum. The Feldmans sat in the center section. He spotted Cantor Berkowitz in the back along with all the other band members' parents.

From the wings, Benny saw Sam loft apples, a banana, and a kiwi above his head without a single one hitting the floor. The fruits disappeared into the rafters, only to return miraculously into his waiting hands. Bowing low, he received a standing ovation. Benny marveled at how calmly his younger brother had executed such a flawless routine. His own palms got cold and sweaty just watching him.

"Great job out there!" Benny said as Sam skipped by.

"Thanks," he said, taking a bite out of one of the apples. "Next year—cantaloupes!"

♪

More acts followed. As the show dragged on, Benny's anxiety level grew. He paced back and forth, thinking back to first grade. The sound of exploding balloons rang in his ears.

"And now, Amanda Grayson's Baton-Twirling Tribute to the Fifty States!" Ms. Krumholtz said.

Great. Just what I need right now. Amanda's perfect performance.

Amanda high-stepped on to the stage with John Philip Sousa's "Washington Post March" blasting from the speakers. The red, white, and blue sequins on her majorette costume sparkled in the spotlight. Knee-high gold boots and a tall hat with a platinum eagle glued to the front completed her outfit. She rotated two batons so fast they looked like biplane propellers pulling her across the shiny floor.

Flashing a blinding smile, Amanda tossed a baton

skyward and waited for its return. Nothing. Seconds passed. No baton in sight. Gazing upward, she saw it lodged between a gap in the ceiling tiles, dangling helplessly out of reach.

Giggles erupted from the front row. Amanda pressed on, spinning the other baton while performing cartwheels and a backflip. The chinstrap on her hat loosened, causing the brim to droop over her right eye. The baton in her hand clattered to the floor.

More laughter.

Amanda performed a split and raised both hands as the music ended. As if on cue, the ceiling tiles released the first baton, sending the guided missile straight through the roof of her cardboard hat.

Ms. Krumholtz yanked the curtain closed as waves of laughter rippled through the auditorium. In the wings, students started assigning Amanda nicknames like the Incredible Lightning Rod and the Human Q-Tip. Names that would make her wish she had never picked up a baton.

Benny heard Amanda sobbing. The laughter and the name-calling grew louder and louder. A voice deep inside him swelled until he was no longer able to hold it in. "STOP IT!" Benny screamed. "STOP IT! STOP IT! STOP IT!"

The chatter ceased. All eyes turned to Benny. He stared back at his classmates, unflinching.

"Tomorrow, Amanda will be called Amanda. And the next day. And the day after that. Nothing more! Got it?"

No one said a word.

"DO YOU UNDERSTAND?" Benny yelled. "HER NAME IS AMANDA!"

"Quiet down, please. People can hear you," Ms. Krumholtz said, putting a finger to her lips.

Benny didn't care. He hoped everyone heard him. Everyone.

In an instant, Benny amended his new rule for getting through the day: Enjoy the ride, but break the speed limit when necessary.

"Are you okay, B-Man?" Jennifer asked.

"Yes, never felt better."

Actually, I feel like throwing up.

♪

Raucous cheers greeted the Neanderthal Four as the curtain opened. To Benny's surprise, there was no billowing fog or artificial wind. Just the four band members and their instruments.

Holding his guitar aloft, Jason strutted to the microphone. "I wrote this song for my dad, Captain Aaron Conroy. Stand up, Dad."

Captain Conroy rose and waved to Jason, who gave a smile, not the smirk Benny was used to seeing.

Illuminated by a single spotlight, Jason launched into a blistering guitar solo lasting for a full minute. Sticks McCracken pounded the drums as if he were furious at the sight of them. The bass guitar and synthesizer turned the song into a swirl of ear-splitting mayhem. Students rushed the stage and bounded up and down like pogo sticks. They smashed into each other, creating a human demolition derby in the auditorium.

The pulsing bass rattled Benny's rib cage. The final piercing guitar note and drum flourish went straight to his brain. The synthesizer made the hairs on his neck stand on end. The roar of the crowd practically brought him to his knees.

Exiting the stage, the Neanderthal Four glided past the Klez Misfits. Jason flicked his guitar pick at Benny.

"Top that," he said.

♫ 30 ♫

"We're on in three minutes! Let's go!" Benny said.

Behind the curtain, Jennifer pushed her drum kit into place. Stuart chewed a fresh wad of Bazooka gum and readjusted his fedora. Royce silently fingered his clarinet's silver keys. Benny tacked up the banner and assumed his position front and center.

Benny's heart pounded. In his mind he pictured an enthusiastic but nasal-clogged boy wrapped in felt, ready to dazzle the world.

"This is it, folks," Royce said. "S-H-O-W-T-I-M-E!"

"We've got this," Stuart said.

"Let's play like our lives depend on it—every note," Benny said, his voice cracking. He felt Uncle Maxwell's quarter which he had placed in his pants pocket for luck.

"Hey, how do you make a Flying V guitar sound even better?" Jennifer asked.

"A joke? Now?" Stuart said.

"How do you make a Flying V guitar sound even better?" she repeated.

"How?" Benny asked.

"Trade it in for a fiddle," Jennifer replied.

"Or an accordion!" Stuart exclaimed.

"Or a clarinet," Royce added.

"Or a drummer who can sing in Yiddish," Benny said.

The band were smiling as the curtain went up.

♪

"For our final act, give a warm welcome to the Klez Misfits!" Ms. Krumholtz said.

A drizzle of applause met the band, mostly from family and friends. The echo of Jason's guitar still resonated off the walls.

Sweaty and tired from jumping around to the Neanderthal Four, students sat with arms folded—silent and skeptical— at the sight of four fedora-wearing musicians.

Benny saw it in their hungry eyes. *Amanda was their appetizer. We're the main course.*

He lifted his bow and closed his eyes. He envisioned his great-great-grandfather pressing down on the strings, carving black ruts into the tips of his fingers. His first note produced the cry from a child strewn with popped purple balloons. He dug in harder until the fiddle moaned. The sound of mourning hung like a low rain cloud over the auditorium.

He opened his eyes to see his mother and father dabbing away tears. Sitting beside one another, Uncle Maxwell and Alistair seemed lost in a distant memory. Students in the first rows yawned and stared blankly at their phones. A voice in the back shouted, "What is this?" Another called out, "Grape alert!" A wadded-up paper landed at Benny's feet.

Benny stood tall. *Not this time. We've come too far.* He focused on Moshe's words: *If you can move one person, you have done your job.*

But beneath the hot lights, the band proceeded with caution, scared of making a mistake. Benny sensed it—everyone was tense, uncertain, wandering through unknown territory. The freedom they had felt in Alistair's Oddities had disappeared. Benny glanced over at the wings where Jason and his band were congratulating each other.

That's when Benny heard it.

One person clapping in rhythm.

Royce's clarinet harmonized with the fiddle on the melody while Stuart squeezed out chords underneath. Jennifer added taps on the snare that gradually became the chug of a locomotive gathering steam.

As more people joined in, the clapping got louder. The band hurtled forward, trading complicated solos, blending in counter-melodies, and taking the tune in directions it had never gone before.

When "Tantz, Tantz Yiddelech" reached maximum

speed, the entire audience was on its feet—clapping and swaying and dancing—from the first row all the way to the back. Benny scanned the sea of people. There was Karen, Alistair, cousins Sara and Jordan, his parents, Uncle Maxwell, Cantor Berkowitz, and classmates who only knew him by one awful name—all vigorously pounding hands together—*as one.*

When the tune ended, the crowd erupted in applause louder than anything Benny had ever imagined. Breathless, the Klez Misfits took a bow and prepared to leave the stage.

But the rhythmic clapping continued. A chant started in the back row and rolled in waves to the front: "ONE MORE SONG! ONE MORE SONG! ONE MORE SONG!"

Principal Dobkins seized the microphone. "Thank you, Klez Misfits. Please exit the stage."

"ONE MORE SONG! ONE MORE SONG! ONE MORE SONG!"

"Sorry, folks, five minutes per group. Those are the rules," he shouted.

Benny glanced at Jennifer. She moved her snare drum to the front.

"This is your final warning. Leave. The. Stage!"

Benny caught a glimpse of Uncle Maxwell, who was giving him two thumbs-up.

"Let's do it," Stuart urged.

"This is too cool!" Royce said.

Enjoy the ride, but break the speed limit when necessary, Benny thought.

Jennifer stared wide-eyed at the standing crowd, frozen and dry-mouthed. Benny slipped his hand into hers and whispered, "You *can* do this, J-Kom. You *can* do this." She banged out four crushing hits on the snare and began singing.

By the time Jennifer reached the chorus, Ms. Krumholtz had forced Principal Dobkins on stage to jitterbug with her.

To Sam's dismay, his parents were dancing the funky chicken—*in ... front ... of ... EVERYBODY.*

Students rushed to the front of the stage. Jason's parents did the twist. Ollie led a conga line around the perimeter of the auditorium with Alistair, Royce's mother, and Cantor Berkowitz bringing up the rear. Uncle Maxwell and Stuart's mother spun around arm in arm. Jennifer's mother sang along as her father drummed his hands on the chair in front of him.

With hands locked together, Benny swung Jennifer in a circle as Royce and Stuart continued playing.

The band held the final note until the audience, exhausted, could not dance another step.

Backstage, Sam hugged his brother. "You guys totally rocked!" he said.

Stuart corrected him. "No, we klezmerized 'em!"

"Is that even a word?" Royce asked.

"It is now," Benny said. "It is now."

♫ **31** ♫

All the acts returned to center-stage where Ms. Krumholtz held the final results. She stood beside a table with three trophies, each topped with a gold-colored microphone.

"How about a big round of applause for all of our participants?" she said.

Hoots and whistles filled the auditorium.

"And now for our top three finishers."

Jennifer gripped Benny's hand.

"In third place—Shiver Me Shakespeare!"

Stuart shot a confident look at Benny, as if to say, "There's *no way* we don't take home the big prize."

Ms. Krumholtz paused for dramatic effect. "And … in second place—Sam Feldman's Flying Fruits."

Sam raced to the front of the stage and held the trophy above his head.

Way to go, Sam, Benny thought. *That's my brother!*

Ollie said what all the Klez Misfits were thinking: "That leaves one spot and two bands. How is that possible?"

Benny smiled. "Don't worry. It will all work out in the end."

Jennifer tightened her hold on his hand.

"And—for the second year in a row—our first-place winner—the Neanderthal Four!"

Jason accepted the prize for the band. Benny shrugged. After the Klez Misfits' performance, he didn't need a trophy to tell him they had played well and that his life would never be the same.

"We've been ripped off!" Stuart said. "We're not even in the top three!"

Royce tried to calm him down. "Remember, we did it R-I-G-H-T. Everybody won here tonight."

Benny took out his quarter and flipped it in the air. "So what do you say? Practice at Alistair's next week?"

"Wouldn't miss it," Royce said.

"Not for the world," Jennifer chimed in.

"We'll see, but probably N-O-T. Just kidding," Stuart joked.

♪

Benny sat in the wings, his fiddle case on his lap. His thoughts reeled back to the Sunday school play. The cast had walked past him without uttering a word. This time, performers from the talent show had a lot to say.

"Man, you can really play!"

"Nice job, Benny."

"Cool band. Cool music."

"Where have you been hiding all these years?"

Then Benny looked up and saw Amanda. Her eyes were puffy from crying. He was surprised that she had stayed around until the end.

"I hope everyone remembers your performance and forgets mine," she said.

"I hope so, too."

"Thanks for standing up for me."

"You're welcome."

"I don't think I would have done the same for you." She looked down at her majorette boots. "I was the one who glued—"

Benny stopped her. "Maybe you will next time."

"Maybe," she said, walking away.

"See you in homeroom tomorrow, AMANDA."

Jason walked up, clutching the trophy. Benny remembered what Jason had said after the play: "I'll never let you forget this." This wasn't going to be a problem with the school talent show. Benny would remember this night—himself—forever.

"I found out your band was disqualified for going over five minutes," Jason said. "Otherwise, you would have won."

Benny was taken aback by the calm tone of Jason's voice. He had expected a snarky rendition of "We Are the Champions" and a new nickname like the "Klez Losers."

"Thanks for letting me know. I guess that's show business," he said.

"I talked with the Neanderthal Four. We agreed the Klez Misfits deserved first place. You were great." Jason handed Benny the trophy.

"So were you."

As Jason turned to walk away, Benny called out, "It was nice to see your father. He must have been proud."

"Thanks, Benny. See ya around."

≥ ♫ ≤

Benny caught up with the Klez Misfits in the school's atrium as friends and family gathered around the band.

"What's with the trophy?" Stuart asked.

"Jason gave it to me. He said even though we had been disqualified, we deserved to win." Each band member took turns holding it.

"I know music isn't about winning, but this will make a nice memory," Benny said.

For once, Royce could not think of a word to describe how he felt. Instead, he talked about adding a full list of songs to the band's repertoire. "Don't forget the *Batman* theme. With plenty of *dreydlekh*! Hey, I'm not kidding."

Stuart looked forward to visiting his father in New Orleans at the end of the school year. "I'm going to bring a little klezmer to Bourbon Street. And Dad and I have a dodgeball game to finish."

Ollie was envisioning cover art for a Klez Misfits

album. He was also thinking that maybe it was time to download some klezmer tunes onto his phone.

Jennifer planned on starting singing lessons. She had also been saving a special joke for after the show.

"What kind of music is scary for balloons?"

Benny had heard this one a hundred times. From now on the answer would never bother him.

"Pop music," he said, smiling.

Benny was already considering the band's next gig. *Maybe at the synagogue? Or a concert at Alistair's to thank him for his friendship?*

But tonight, do I have a story to tell Moshe!

Klezmer Terms

Ahava Raba: Scale used in many klezmer and non-Jewish folk songs; it means "great love" in Hebrew.

Bulgar: Up-tempo dance with a syncopated rhythm; it was known as *bulgarish* in Eastern Europe and renamed *bulgar* in America.

Doina: Improvised lament usually performed solo and often played as an introduction to a dance tune.

Dreydlekh: Musical ornamentation, such as sliding notes, used to breathe life into klezmer tunes.

Freylekh: Joyful circle dance; it means "festive" in Yiddish.

Krecht: Wailing, sobbing note.

Mazurka: Lively Polish dance.

Sher: Moderate-tempo square dance.

Abe Schwartz's Orchestra: Abraham Schwartz (1881–1963) was a noted klezmer fiddler, pianist, composer, and bandleader who moved to the United States from Romania in 1899. As leader of his klezmer orchestra, he recorded many tunes in America, including "Tantz, Tantz Yiddelech" and "Unser Toirele," both referenced in the book.

Authors' Note

"All music is connected ... and music connects us all."

Many musicians, bands, and composers fill the pages of this book. They represent the diverse landscape of music, from classical composer Maurice Ravel to modern-day pop star Pink. You can take your own musical journey by learning about the different musicians and compositions mentioned throughout the text, just as Benny does during his violin lessons with Uncle Maxwell. Listen for the joy or sorrow of each piece. Hear how jazz, klezmer, and classical music share a common language. Treat your ears to something new—maybe a didgeridoo concert or some Cajun accordion. Who knows? You may end up like Ollie and decide it's time to load a few klezmer tunes onto your phone!

≥ ♪ ≤

Acknowledgments

Like a klezmer ensemble coming together to make music, it takes many different players to orchestrate a book. We would like to express our sincere thanks to our fellow "band" members for helping to bring Benny's story to life: Catriella Freedman and the dedicated staff at PJ Our Way; Michael Leventhal of Green Bean Books; Jessica Cuthbert-Smith and her production team; our readers, Lisa Bansen-Harp, Rita Marks, and Lois Reaven; and our loving family who encouraged us along the way.

Other Green Bean Books

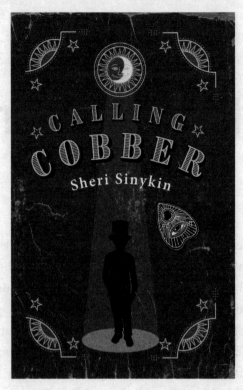

Sometimes it seems as if there's too much for eleven-year-old Jacob 'Cobber' Stern to worry about, and his workaholic father doesn't seem to notice.

He misses his mom, he feels abandoned by his best friend Boolkie, who is studying for his bar mitzvah, and his greatgrandfather Papa-Ben is nearly a hundred years old and struggling to live on his own.

As Cobber tackles these challenges he learns more about the people around him: why his father works so hard, why Papa Ben doesn't want to talk to his class at school, and why Boolkie wants to have a bar mitzvah. The results are funny and moving as Cobber begins to understand about the threads that bind them all together.

GOING
ROGUE
(AT HEBREW SCHOOL)

CASEY BRETON

Ten-year-old Avery Green has always hated Hebrew School. And why shouldn't he? Not only does it mean he has to spend extra time inside of a classroom, but also Hebrew school has absolutely nothing to do with his three most favourite things in the universe: Star Wars, science, and football.

But everything turns upside down the day Avery begins to suspect that the mysterious new rabbi just might happen to be… an actual Jedi master! Armed with nothing more than a curious mind and an endless supply of questions, Avery sets out to reveal the truth about Rabbi Bob.

Join Avery as he finds friendship in the most unlikely of places and discovers that people are not always as they first appear.

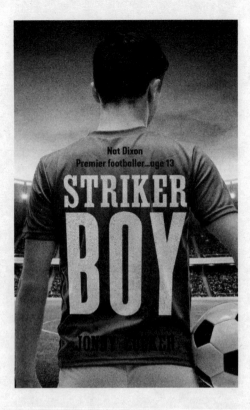

Nat Dixon
Premier footballer...age 13

STRIKER
BOY

Just a few days after Nat Levy's thirteenth birthday, he and his dad Dave return to England for the first time in seven years. Since his mother died, the two of them have been travelling from country to country, wherever Dave can pick up work, and Nat has been playing street football with the local kids whenever he has a chance – even on Copa Cabana beach in Rio de Janeiro!

With the shock to being back to England, the only positive aspect is that they are close to Hatton Rangers, the football club they both follow, but the club is struggling to avoid relegation and possible bankruptcy. Amazingly, Nat's football skills are spotted and he is put forward for a trial at the club. However, there is something fishy going on at the club that is looking increasingly dangerous...